A Dog's Hope

A Dog's
Hope

CASEY WILSON

bookouture

Published by Bookouture in 2020

An imprint of Storyfire Ltd.
Carmelite House
50 Victoria Embankment
London EC4Y 0DZ

www.bookouture.com

Written by Casey Wilson

ISBN: 978-1-83888-102-3
eBook ISBN: 978-1-83888-101-6

This book is a work of fiction. Names, characters, businesses, organizations, places and events other than those clearly in the public domain, are either the product of the author's imagination or are used fictitiously. Any resemblance to actual persons, living or dead, events or locales is entirely coincidental.

In memory of Zoe, who will always have a place in my heart

CHAPTER 1

Now

With a gentle touch, Karen runs her hand over my back, sluicing the rainwater off my fur. "Buddy, please come home with me." She sighs and blows her nose. "It's getting late and it's too cold. I need to go."

I move my eyes to meet hers, but my chin remains on the cold flat stone etched with letters. Rain doesn't bother me. Cold weather doesn't bother me. My golden fur is thick and protects me from the elements. Even snow can't penetrate it. I can roll in it for hours, using my nose to make a tunnel in fresh fallen snow. It makes me sneeze, but it's *so* worth it.

I notice Karen's pleading look. She has to realize I can't leave. I'm waiting for Toby. As long as it takes. I beg her to see this with my eyes. Toby always understands me; we've never needed words.

Karen shivers as she dabs at her cheeks, but kneels down in her dress on the wet grass. She steadies the umbrella over both of us as she places a tender hand on my head, using her thumb to pet the corner of my ear. "I know you don't understand, but he's gone. Our boy isn't coming home."

Karen has always had a gentle voice, but it breaks as she murmurs to me. I detect her scent—lavender. She always smells of it. Soft and calm. I lick her hand and she rewards me with a caress of my graying muzzle. Tears drop from her eyes and land on my paw.

Karen says we have to say goodbye to Toby today, but it doesn't make sense to me. I nose closer to the worn leather baseball mitt resting atop the stone, the familiar smells of leather, oil, and dirt mingle with my favorite scent—Toby.

How many times have I rested my chin in the palm of that glove and looked at Toby's face? I shut my eyes and let the scent take me back to the field on our way home. Toby and I cross the skinny ribbon of water that runs alongside of it and have the whole green pasture to ourselves. Mounds of dirt dot the sturdy grass, but I don't let the enticing scent distract me. My sole focus is my boy and our game.

I wonder how Toby came up with such a clever way for us to spend time together, but I'll be forever grateful for it. It's more than a simple game. It's our connection. I hear the thwack of the ball in his hand as he prepares to throw it, and in his eyes when they meet mine, I can see we're alone in the world, just the two of us. There's a glimmer when he's about to release the ball, but I keep my eye on the white sphere and I know it's coming. As soon as he lets it fly, I rush to snag it before it hits the ground.

I detect all of Toby's scents on the ball. Pencil lead, paper, the burrito he had for lunch, the sweat on his palms, the citrus aroma of his hair gel, all of them combined together smell like my boy. I make a beeline for him. My eyes focus only on him and his smile urges me forward. There's no time to think when you're staring into your best friend's eyes, waiting for the next ball.

Karen's sobs interrupt my memories. Her sorrow surrounds her like a mist of dark fog. I watch her weep as she moves her hands from me and traces the letters carved in the stone. It makes me want to go home with her and comfort her, but I can't. I whine in sympathy, but don't shift from my position. Toby needs me more. I've always waited for him, ever since we met. I'll wait for him now.

I remember listening to the men in their pristine uniforms and shiny buttons who had arrived at the house. They told Karen how sorry they were that Toby's body still hadn't been recovered; they had lost hope and in turn so did she. If they couldn't find his body, how could they return his remains? I watched her crumple to the floor, her sobs uncontrollable, heart-wrenching, and my licks did little to console her.

At first, she was like me, she refused to believe. Since the day the men came, she hasn't been able to work. Instead, I comfort her as she sits on the bench in the backyard overlooking her beloved flowers. She strokes my back for hours on end as she struggles to accept the news. She sips cup after cup of tea, and I make sure I'm close to her, so she knows she isn't alone. Unlike me, it's too painful for her to hope, so I'll bear the burden. I'll be the one to wait for Toby. All of her days, recently, have been filled with tears, but today has been her saddest day.

The man who prayed and stood by the stone drove away hours ago. He held Karen's hand and stayed with her long after the men in uniforms had come and gone. My ears still hurt from the sad tones that came from the music one of them had played.

The flag Karen holds crackles as she clutches it against her chest and gets to her feet. Startled by the noise, I raise myself into a sitting position, but make no attempt to stand. She shakes her head and gives me a look I don't see often. Her frustration with me is clear. She thrusts the handle of the umbrella into the wet grass and positions it over me.

It has been a long day. I'm weary with the weight of all of my twelve years bearing down on my tired bones. My eyes grow heavy as I stare at the stone in the midst of the grassy expanse. A breeze tickles my nose and I sniff the air again, but Toby isn't here.

Karen walks away, through the wet grass, and I shut my eyes.

The crunch of her footsteps on the asphalt pathway wake me, and I have no idea how long she's been gone. She's concealed under a bright yellow raincoat, trudging across the grass, carrying an armful of stuff from her car: a bowl of food and one for water.

"You need to eat, Buddy. Please." Tears dot her cheeks. "I can't lose you too." She puts a piece of my favorite pumpkin cookie treat next to my mouth and I remember the first one Toby ever bought me. I recognize the thick bone-shaped confection, drizzled with yogurt glaze. They're crunchy on the outside, softer on the inside and have a spicy flavor that always makes me drool. My nose draws in the comforting scent of cinnamon, nutty flour and egg; the mellow aroma of pumpkin softens the savory peanut butter scent. My nose twitches, my body's urge to leap for a bite is overwhelming and I can't help the drool forming in my mouth. Natural instincts are hard to control; our instincts are so deep, we cannot resist them.

Since Toby's been gone, Karen's taken to baking me treats. I love licking the bowl after she's scooped out all the batter. Pre-washing—that's my job. Each night after dinner I take up my appointed position in front of the dishwasher. Karen gives some of the plates a cursory rinse, but I handle the rest. I run my tongue over all the silverware and get any stray food from between the tines of the forks. My favorite nights are the ones when she uses the outdoor grill. She never rinses the platter and I relish the juice and bits of meat that are always leftover.

She looks so sad, I take the treat from the ground and that, at least, makes her smile, just for a moment.

She tugs on my collar. "Can you get up, Buddy?"

I'm too tired to comply. She walks back to her car and returns with one of my old beds. The rain has stopped and she removes her hood while she puts down a ratty towel on the grass and positions my bed. "Get on the bed, Buddy. Come on, be a good boy."

I recognize the worry she's feeling. She reeks of sorrow and despair and I don't want to cause her anymore grief than she has already endured. I struggle to raise myself. She bends and helps me, placing her soft hands—the hands that always smell like flowers—under me and heaves to help me stand. I shake and release a cascade of water to splatter over her.

She squeals, but grins. "Good boy, Buddy. I understand you want to stay here. I just want you protected. Toby would want you safe. He would never forgive me if something happened to you."

I follow her gesture and ease back down on the bed. She uses another towel to dry my fur and I let her continue, even though I know my thick coat will endure the water. I know it makes her feel better, so I indulge her. The massage she's giving me is soothing; it warms my muscles and relaxes them. The pressure of her hands on my back feels wonderful and I sense her touch lighten when she gets to my hips. My eyes are getting heavy as she continues to dry my belly, so I let them close and pretend it's Toby drying me off after a bath. He'd let me wallow on the grass to dry my fur and then use a towel to finish off. I'd let him almost complete the task and then lunge and grab the towel in my teeth. He'd tug on it and we'd go back and forth. There's nothing like the satisfying sound of a towel splitting between my teeth—the fibers as they strain, desperate to keep together, and the sudden break sending us both across the lawn. Plus, it was an easy way to identify which towels were mine.

She makes another pass over me and presses too hard on my hip, sending a jolt of pain through me. I flinch and lift my head. It only hurts if I stay in one place too long and I haven't moved much today. I should walk more, but I can't. "I'm sorry, Buddy." She rests her cheek against my back and pets my ears. The pain subsides.

She moves Toby's glove so it's near my head. "There you go. Now you'll be off of the wet grass tonight. The rain is over so you won't get wet." She covers me with a blanket I recognize from the back of her car.

"One night, Buddy. I'll be back in the morning and we'll go home, okay? I have to go to work this week and I don't want to worry about you."

I don't commit. I'll come home when Toby does. Karen leans over and kisses the top of my head before she makes her way to her car.

The old bed makes a far more comfortable spot than the ground. Since Toby left last year, it has been getting harder for me to stand. I have a difficult time finding a comfortable position and have to move often. Karen added soft rugs to the hardwood floors where I like to rest, making it easier for me to gain a foothold.

When Toby was home we exercised and played each day, so maybe I didn't notice my hip much. Now, Karen takes me for walks near our house, but my heart isn't in it. It's not the same as when Toby and I play together. My favorite person, my purpose, is missing.

It's quiet here, except for the soft rustle of the trees in the breeze and the scuttle of squirrels in search of food. I watch them dart close to my food bowl and then scamper away in distress. The squirrels are wary, but have nothing to fear. I'm in no shape to chase them.

I pretend I'm asleep and let them get closer. There are two of them, less than a foot away from me, rummaging through my bowl, gathering bites of my kibble. With a swift motion, I raise my head and watch them scurry away, cheeks full. A dog has to have a little fun. Even an old dog.

The view from the grassy hill I'm on is idyllic. The valley below is dotted with the farms and orchards Toby and I walked by each day. With a slight turn of my head I take in the shimmering water of the lake in the center of town. I love walking along the path by the lake with Toby. When he comes back, he'll take me there again.

I know Toby wouldn't leave me. He told me he'd be back and he keeps his promises.

I lift my head again and gaze across the grass, admiring the huge trees. It's quiet and peaceful. I've never been here during the time I've lived with Toby and Karen.

The breeze carries the scent of apples. Along with the crunch of a few leaves falling from the trees, this delicious sweet aroma announces the arrival of fall in Riverside. It's my favorite time of year and the perfect weather for a golden retriever with a heavy coat like mine. Toby and I liked to watch apples fall from the trees along our walk to and from school. He would always scoop one of them up as it rested on the ground, shimmering red amongst the grass and bite chunks off for me on our way home from practice or games.

Toby and I missed baseball season again this year. I reposition his glove with my snout and place my head on the rubbed and scarred leather. As I sniff his scent, imbedded in the laces and webbing, I let my mind wander to Toby's games. I never knew much about the sport until I met Toby and spent so much time watching him practice and play, listening as the coach gave directions. I learned it's much more than just a game.

Baseball teaches humans to be more like dogs; to live in the moment. I learned that quickly, but Toby took a little longer to understand. "It ain't over till it's over," Coach used to say.

I know it's not over for Toby. Baseball teaches you not to give up and I'm not giving up on Toby. I'm hoping for one more inning.

I reposition myself and exhale a long breath. I have to admit, this old bed isn't bad. I would always try to stay on the rug beside Toby's bed, but from the first night he let me snuggle under the covers with him.

Toby's my everything.

CHAPTER 2

Then

Mom's heavy sigh when I put the gearshift in park makes me turn my head. "Really? I'm not that bad of a driver, am I?" I resist the urge to roll my eyes.

She chuckles and shakes her head. "No, you did a fine job, especially for someone who's not been driving for very long. I'm just tired." She heaves her purse from the floor and retrieves the keys to our new house, looking still, for a moment, as she surveys the front. I stare at the rather plain-looking tan exterior trimmed in white. It's smaller than our old house, single-story, instead of the two-story house we left, with nothing but vacant land and a few rolling hills behind it. The house is on a large plot of land, at least a quarter of an acre. A new wooden fence surrounds the property, with a gate to the backyard. The front yard is planted with grass, but it's dormant and brown, with just a couple of evergreen bushes decorating the bare flowerbeds. The house next door has a realtor sign in front of it and I can see that the lot on the other side of us is empty.

I can't imagine cramming all of our stuff from our old house into this space. In the car, Mom chattered on about the house being brand new and how nice it would be not to have to worry about maintenance, but I know she sees more than this: peace and quiet, serenity. The first house she's ever owned on her own.

"I'll unlock the doors. Could you move the van and back it up to the garage door to make it easier to unload?" she says, brushing a hand against my shoulder.

My jaw tenses but I stop myself asking Mom why she couldn't have told me that before I parked. I'm tired and I know she is too from staying up late and packing last night. I'm not in the mood to listen to anymore lectures about turning over a new leaf or keeping on the right path. Sometimes I think she forgets I'm not one of her students. I reposition the old silver vehicle she has driven for years and I get out to start unloading boxes as she steps inside the garage.

"The movers have all the furniture placed. At least the heavy stuff is done," she says, poking her head from under the garage door as it rises, and I survey the stacks of boxes left by the movers that cover almost the whole floor of the space barely big enough for a single car. Our old house had an oversized garage that housed two cars and still had room left over for storage.

"Do you want all these moved into the house?" I ask.

"No, let's work on the stuff we brought in the van first." She gives me directions based on the labels attached to each box and leads the way into the house. "You can pick from the two bedrooms. I thought you'd probably want the bigger one. It will get less morning sun," she says. It may be her house but of course she doesn't come first. Mom has always been like this, leading the way, unselfishly sacrificing her needs for mine: serving my food before her own, making sure the tears in my jeans are sewn before she moves on to her dresses with her battered wooden sewing box.

When we left Seattle this morning it was overcast and drizzling. It's chilly here, but the sun is shining and I feel the warmth on my back as I collect the boxes and bring them inside. Mom said we would get less rain in this part of the state, along with more snow in the winter and heat in the summer, explaining it as if it mattered much to me. I had no choice in moving here. I follow her inside to check out the house.

It's super clean and smells new, with that slight chemical odor that accompanies new carpet and new cars. I step through the tiled utility room off the garage and notice the cheap, imitation wood flooring. It's an open design with a large space in the middle of the house that serves as the living, kitchen, and small dining area. Mom leads me on a tour and shows me the spare bedroom choices, on either side of a bathroom. The bedrooms aren't carpeted, but I take the bigger one, like she suggested. There's no point in arguing with her today.

Mom's master bedroom is a little larger than mine, but nothing special and her bathroom is a definite downgrade from her old one with double sinks and a walk-in shower. I wander back to the main area, taking in our old battered furniture that has been put in place and look out of the sliding glass doors to the patio and yard in the back of the house. There's nothing behind us, just a view of the hills and some open space. Nothing like the city, where there were houses in every direction, people watching us from all sides, thousands of neighbors to avoid getting to know.

I start unpacking my stuff while Mom works in the kitchen, opening the flimsy-looking blinds to let more light into the room, giving me a view into the backyard. I unload dusty books I've never read and framed photos of me as a little kid with Mom and Dad. We're all smiling in the photos, but that was a long time ago. There are no recent photos of our happy family in the house, no other trips to the zoo or drives down to the ocean. I'm not sure you can include someone in your family if they're never around.

For a while now, Mom's life has only consisted of me and her work. She grades papers, struggles to make sure things are done around the house. I've never seen her go out with friends or do anything fun, but her demeanor is beginning to change, her body relaxing, as though getting out of the city has already made a difference to her, and I hope it lasts. We're always moving, always starting again, I don't feel like we ever stay in one place for long.

I have a ton of books for a guy who doesn't even like them. Mom used to read to me each night before I went to bed, but as I shelve them all, I wonder why I'm keeping them. They're for little kids but I'm sure Mom doesn't want to part with them. She's always recommending something for me to read. She brought all the Harry Potter books home for me when I was younger and stacked them in my room, but after the dust piled up on them, she finally figured out I wasn't interested.

I put my clothes in the closet, fill my dresser and wiggle the worn drawers closed, noticing a new deep scratch in the already marred top, and look at the rolled-up posters I had on the walls in my other room and pause. I'm not sure I want to put them up.

There's a wooden box with my old rock collection. I used to think that every rock had been on its own journey, had a history worth saving, from the smooth pebbles that had been abraded by rivers to the ones covered in limestone that looked like crystal. I was obsessed, but I haven't added to the box for years.

There's another box filled with the models of cars and planes I built when I was fourteen. The ones that survived me flinging them across the room when I got so mad about Dad. Why has Mom bothered to pack these? Protecting each one with bubble wrap to care for the fragile wings. I remember getting these from Dad, and his promise to build them with me, but I could never get him to.

I slam the lid back on the box and stuff it on the top shelf of my closet. There's no point in displaying them. I add the box of rocks to the shelf in the closet, toss my shoes inside, and shut the door.

I thumb through a short stack of postcards Dad sent to me over the years of his military career. He never says much, just a line about making sure I behave and take care of Mom. I toss them across the room into a box of trash. They're just a reminder of our lack of a relationship. Distant, brief, and without any real meaning, just one-way orders barked at me, whether he's here or halfway across the world.

I sit on my mattress and look around my new space. It's sparse, there's no denying that the bookshelves look empty without the models. But empty is better than staring at stuff I don't care about anymore.

I haul the empty boxes back to the garage and flatten them for recycling, and the sound of cupboard doors opening and closing leads me to the kitchen.

"OK?" Mom asks softly as I stand in the doorway.

I notice how tired she looks, how she still strokes the skin on her finger where her ring used to be. She's been packing our house for weeks, staying up late each night and I haven't been much help.

"It's a nice house," I say, trying to bridge the gap that's widened between us these past few months. "Has a great yard and it's smaller, but seems bigger."

She laughs and ruffles my hair, like she has done since I was a little kid. "I know it's not as nice as our old house." She pauses. "I like the open design." I know she wants to put her arm around my shoulders. "I think we're going to like it here," she says tentatively.

I look out the window into the yard and the open space beyond. I've left everything I know behind. It's not that I was that attached to my school, or my friends, but at least they were familiar.

All I can hear is my stomach rumbling, gurgling from deep within like I haven't eaten in months. The trip from Seattle took a little over three hours and we've been working for a few more.

"Shall we get some lunch?" I ask Mom, whose attention lasted only a moment with me before it went back to the crockery jumbled in boxes.

She glances at her watch. "Sure, let's see what we can find."

"Fast-food works. Niko's for a gyro? Peso's Tacos would be good. Even Seoul Bowl for Korean." I watch her face fall. "Shake Shack?" I ask with desperation.

Mom pokes buttons on her phone and scrolls her screen. "Sorry, not much in the way of chain options here."

"Great." My sarcasm is obvious—it earns me a disapproving grimace. A few weeks ago, I wouldn't have dreamed of going out with Mom. I was always too busy doing everything I could to avoid her, but here, in this new town, even if I'm not sure about fresh starts, even if this is only for a few months, I should at least make an effort to forget the past. I'm so hungry my stomach is on fire and I shrug. "It's fine. Let's just go and find someplace. How hard can it be in a town this size?"

*

Mom slides behind the wheel and steers in the direction of the heart of Riverside. The wide streets give way to our route alongside fields. Traffic is nonexistent. Nothing like the crowded narrow streets in the city.

As I take in the expanse of open space, I look at the choices on my phone. I can tell that Mom is frazzled from the move and the divorce; we've had a lot of stuff going on recently—phone calls with real estate agents, organizing our belongings, saying goodbye to the people we'd grown close to. "How about a place called Two Sisters?" I say and give her directions.

Our new house is in a little avenue called Hillview, less than a mile from the main street that runs through the town. It's a tiny little thing but it looks like there are huge houses in the town: types with white picket fences, beautiful manicured lawns. I didn't know Mom had even been looking to move here until she told me she'd got the job. With all her enthusiasm, her positivity about a fresh start, I couldn't bear to let her down, to tell her it was all a bit sudden. That maybe I didn't want to move. That maybe this was one too many changes. But she said the job she found was perfect for her, that the town was what a "growing boy needs" and I knew I'd have to go anyway.

She's replacing a teacher who has moved, so she's stepping into an already established classroom of fourth graders come Monday morning, and I assume they're not paying her much. Hanging around with young kids all day sounds like a nightmare to me—I've never really been around young children, since I don't have any siblings, any cousins, much family—but Mom loves her job. She said she's happy she doesn't have to start from scratch as far as setting up the classroom.

She pours her heart and soul into her job—is always getting gifts and cards from parents and students. She has a habit of inviting them to the house—as if she picks out the most vulnerable ones, those who may not have the best home life. She'll make them a meal, help them with their studies, and shower them with school supplies or educational games. She's constantly baking treats or making platters of healthy snacks to take to them. At times I'm almost jealous at the amount of attention she pays them. But it's fine, I shouldn't need her anymore.

We pass by a sign: "Downtown Riverside" and I eye the main street with its perfect-looking little shops under green awnings. There are a handful of cars parked along the side and a few people on the sidewalk, but other than that it's deserted. A white gazebo dominates a large square in the center of town and colorful banners attached to the old-fashioned light poles advertise local attractions. I'm not sure it even qualifies as a town. It's more like a village. I laugh. "This is downtown?"

Mom shakes her head and her shoulders slump. "Give it a chance, Toby." I keep quiet but don't like the odds of finding much to do here. Mom's pleas for me to take this move seriously have been getting more and more impassioned, and now we're here I know she's not going to give up. At least I can try.

But can I erase my entire past? Keep it from the people in town? Can she erase her own?

CHAPTER 3

The ladies behind the counter are friendly and give us a few minutes to make our choices, but it isn't hard: soup, a handful of sandwiches, a few salads, and lots of coffee and tea drinks, those are all the options we have. I've never understood small town life; how you can see the same people every day, choose from the same menu, which never changes.

I opt for the soup and roast beef and take a seat while Mom pays. The ladies laugh and chat with her and I hear Mom's upbeat voice introducing herself—the voice of a teacher. Warm and caring, friendly, but with an authority that comes from years of teaching fourth graders, whose moods and whims are constantly changing.

"… at Riverside Elementary," Mom says, and the women turn and look in my direction as she gestures my way. "That's my son, Toby. He's a sophomore in high school."

"It's like a real-life Mayberry," I say, under my breath as I shake my head. I look up and return a smile to the two ladies working the counter.

In Seattle nobody knew us. Nobody chatted like this. Baristas were in a hurry and wanted you to move along and make room for the next guy. Pay for your stuff and get out of the way, no chitchat, and that suited me fine.

Riverside, it appears, is the chitchat capital of Washington. While Mom visits, I have time to study the place. Local happenings plaster the old brick wall, and brochures tucked in a rack promise tourists fun adventures. Fruit orchards, vineyards, lake activities, and golf are my choices for entertainment.

I turn and glance at the wall behind me. It holds a collection of jerseys and pennants from the local middle and high school teams. Team photos and the high school colors of green and gold dominate. Riverside holds the state title in basketball from the 1970s, wrestling for several of the recent years, and baseball for the last ten years. Team schedules are displayed next to the memorabilia.

Mom laughs and grins with the women and her smile even brightens my face. The divorce has been hard on her but I've never been able to understand why she's been so upset about it. I'm not convinced our lives are that different now. Mom tried so hard to make everything work. Anytime Dad was due home, I watched as she hurried through the house, making sure all the furniture and floors gleamed and there wasn't a speck of dust around the place. She cooked his favorite dishes and made sure the kitchen was stocked with some of the snacks he enjoyed. She planned activities and tried to make us a real family when Dad was on leave. When he was away, I'm sure she emailed often and called whenever his schedule was open. I often heard her getting up in the middle of the night. She kept things running in his absence and never complained about being on her own. When he was home, he wasn't easy to be around, but I never heard her complain. Instead, she'd make excuses for him and took whatever steps necessary to ease the turbulence he created.

She's the one who told me they were getting divorced; of course he wasn't present for that conversation. She said she had failed, like it was all on her shoulders. When she explained we had to move because we couldn't stay in the military house, she pretended to be happy. I know she wasn't the one who failed, and I'd rather live anywhere, in any tiny house, move around every year, if it makes her happy.

Dad was never around when we needed him. If we had something break at home, we had to figure it out or call the maintenance crew. If her car had a problem, she had to rely on one of her friends' husbands. I can fix most things, but when I was little, Mom had to find people to help her. I remember we had a huge leak underneath the sink not too long ago. It was in the middle of the night and I found her on the floor, crying, as she tried to turn the valve. She had blisters on her hands from trying to turn it and was using the wrong type of wrench. Panic was written all over her face as she struggled with it and tried to keep the water contained with towels. When I got it shut off, she wrapped her arms around me and smiled through her tears. *I couldn't have managed without you, Toby.*

Dad was always deployed or training. Master Chief Petty Officer William Fuller lives and breathes for the U.S. Navy. It's such a ridiculous title. He's part of the Special Warfare Command Team, supporting the Navy Seals, and he can be spun up at a moment's notice. He can never discuss his work or talk about his missions, but I know from attending some of the ceremonies for Dad's unit, that Dad and his guys get sent to some of the most dangerous areas in the world. Their missions are always secret, and whenever there is television coverage of hostage situations in foreign lands, I know it could be him.

Although we lived next door to other military families, most of them had younger kids with stay-at-home moms, so I had little in common with them. When Dad joined the special team, Mom elected to stay in Seattle, rather than relocate, and we lost most of our connections to the other families of his colleagues. We got to stay in the house, while Dad spent his time on ships or at coastal bases and bunks—heading off wherever the job took him.

Years ago, we used to have weekend barbeques where each of the families on our street would take turns hosting. The dads would set up volleyball nets, horseshoes, and croquet and we'd all play until it was time to eat. Everyone brought food and, in the summer, we'd even have water balloon fights. It was hard to keep friendships, since it seemed like our dads were always being sent to a new base, but I remember some fun times. Mom and Dad were more at ease then, but that was before.

Moving every couple of years always made things difficult.

When I overheard them talking at the end of last summer, I knew it was different this time. I heard my dad's harsh tones—his strong, authoritative voice, the same voice that used to chuckle at the radio on Sunday mornings, that would once hum through dishes on Friday nights.

"The majority of my new training will take place near San Diego. You'll need to pack up the house and be ready to move in a couple of weeks," he'd said in his usual clipped style, without even taking a breath, without even giving Mom a chance to react. "Housing will deliver boxes within three days."

There was no opening for discussion, his words were just another order, like she was in his unit. She didn't raise her voice, but her serious tone revealed her resolve. I had just started down the stairs, but took a step back when her inflection changed and crouched on the landing, where I couldn't be seen. I wedged my head against the old library card catalog Mom kept there and peeked through the balusters to watch them.

"I know this promotion means so much to you," she'd said, cautiously, at first. "You know I'm proud of your work… but I don't think uprooting Toby just as he's going into high school is a good idea. He needs stability and routine. Maybe he and I can stay here while you're on assignment. If the position becomes permanent, we could revisit the idea of moving."

"You're willing to break up our family, so he can go to the same school? Give me a break, Karen. He's not a little kid. You coddle him too much."

Her shoulders slumped and she shook her head as she put her arm around his shoulders. "It's about having a peaceful home. For all of us. I'm worried about you and I don't want to split our family apart, but all this upheaval isn't good, especially for Toby. Something has to change."

Dad was silent for a few minutes, his head downcast. "You think not having me here will solve it all?" These words he uttered quieter, wounded, and I thought he seemed sad…

"That's not at all what I mean, but I don't think you'll see any less of us than you already do, William. My priority is Toby. We've moved with you over the course of your career, more times than I care to admit. I'm tired of moving and Toby doesn't need the turmoil. Teenagers have enough change happening without adding to it, unnecessarily. You know what he's like. Can't you see he's struggling?"

He remained quiet. She took in a deep breath and added, "You wanted this job and only told me after you put in for the promotion. I didn't get a say in that decision. It's your career and your decision. I also have a career here I like, but more than that, our son is my top priority and it's my job to do what's best for him. We're staying here."

"That's great, just great. Makes about as much sense as everything else here," Dad had shouted and left, slamming the door so hard the windows vibrated.

She didn't cry, just went back to grading her papers. I let out the breath I had been holding and felt relief. I'm not sure I remember a time when she didn't just cave to whatever Dad wanted. He was always a dominant force and she submitted to his demands. A sense of pride swelled up in me. It was a good plan, with the best of intentions, but she had no idea they'd soon get divorced.

Whenever Dad was home, he was always restless. If I tried to ask him questions, he'd snap at me and tell me he couldn't talk.

When I was a kid, I remember having fun with him and how we played backgammon all the time. We loved that game and kept score in a notebook, like a perpetual tournament. While Mom was grading papers, we'd spend time moving the black and white pieces around the board. Things had changed, though. Lately, when we tried to do things together, it always ended in an argument. Now, I'm not even sure he really knows me anymore. We don't have many shared interests, and just fake our way through trying to do things together for the few days when he's home on leave.

The furrows of his brow are forever etched in my mind but I can't say I miss him. I miss the dad he used to be, but lately he hasn't been much of a father and I can't count on him like I can Mom.

Mom deserves better. I know part of the reason she moved us here is because of me, because in the last few months I've spent more time getting into trouble than I have doing anything else.

But Dad's still the biggest reason we're here now. Mom can't afford to live in the city. It's cheaper to live here and it's a new start. For both of us.

Mom arrives with our tray of food. "This looks good, huh?"

I nod and grab my sandwich. As I eat, Mom rambles on about the women who work here. They both have children in her school and the one named Molly has a daughter in high school. Molly is the redhead with a sprinkle of freckles across her cheeks and the slimmer of the two women. She and her sister, Ginny, the dark-haired woman with the chubby figure and what looks like a permanent smile, own the place. I finish my lunch and Mom hasn't even eaten half of hers.

Molly walks by our table and places a plate containing two frosted brownies in front of us. She seems so at ease with herself, like she was born in this town, in this café, like she's a part of the fixtures and fittings. "On the house. Just a little welcome to the town," she says, giving me a smile I can't help but reciprocate.

"Thanks, those look good," I say. Mom babbles her appreciation, gushing on and on about how nice it is to be in a small town, before Molly's eyes are back on me.

"I saw you checking out our Riverside pride wall," she says, moving closer to me. She has the deepest dimples in her cheeks I've ever seen. "We're full of spirit when it comes to school sports. It's our little way of paying tribute here at the café."

I nod. Clearly there's not a lot to do in this town.

Ginny wanders over and joins in the conversation, bringing her mug of coffee and the rest of the cookie she was eating, not realizing she's dropping crumbs along the way. "The whole town gets behind the teams and celebrates our wins. It's always been like that. We grew up here."

"You've lived here your whole life?" I ask.

They both bob their heads. "There's a chili feed coming up and a pancake breakfast in a few weeks," Ginny says, counting the events on her fingers with passion. "They're fundraisers for the high school teams. You two should come."

Mom bobs her head up and down, agreeing to what sounds like a complete snore fest to me. If she'd stop jabbering and look at me, she'd know the idea of socializing with the country bumpkins in a stuffy gymnasium is the last thing I want to do. We can make a fresh start as much as we want in this town, but we can't change who we are—what we've been through, where we come from.

The brownies are out of this world and I consider the idea of eating the other one while Mom chats. Would she even notice? She's so entranced by this place, so into her conversation, I doubt she'd notice if I were here at all. After several more minutes, Mom lets Molly and Ginny get back to work and turns her attention to her sandwich. I drum my fingers on the table.

"Let's drive by your school on the way to the house," Mom says, between nibbles. "Since you'll be walking, I want to make sure you're familiar with the route."

She finishes her sandwich, gives me half of her brownie, and waves goodbye to the ladies. "Nice meeting you, Karen. You too, Toby," says Molly.

I nod, give them a wave, and hold the door for Mom.

"Aren't they friendly?" she asks as we take a few steps on the sidewalk.

"They seem nice. The food's good, *especially* the brownies." I shake my head and add, "I can't imagine they've lived here for what, forty-some years?"

"They seem happy enough to me," she says. "We'll have to check out some of those fundraisers. It would be a good way to meet people."

"I guess," I say, with a shrug, not wanting to burst her bubble. Mom always went to social events sponsored by her old school, and not just for her class. She continued to attend plays and performances for kids that had moved on to the upper grades. She seemed to always have three or four students each year that she really clicked with and she made sure to support them and attend their activities. Gavin played the piano and she went to all of his recitals, and sweet little Beth was obsessed with ballet. Mom kept her dance schedule on our refrigerator and made a point of going to her performances. The junior high where most of her students attended had a talent show and a school play each year and, without fail, Mom was in the audience applauding and finding them after the event to dispense praise and hugs.

School was her happy place, but I didn't have an interest in hanging around any longer than I had to and my school didn't offer much in the way of parental involvement. Once you left elementary school and had different teachers all day, the sense of belonging to a classroom faded away. Mom checked my grades online through the parent portal, but parents only came to school if they were summoned by the principal or for sporting events and musicals, and I wasn't into either of those.

She moves her head from side to side taking in the landmarks and points to the street sign. "Lincoln Avenue. This street goes across the lake. There are only two of them that do. Lincoln and Jackson. The high school is on the other side of the lake."

She starts the van and says, "I'll show you my school after we check out yours. It's on Cedar Street on this side."

We putter through the near empty main street and turn to cross over the lake. It's prettier than the photos online. Riverside nestles in a valley that looks like it was scooped out from between the Cascade Mountains and surrounding hills. The town rests at the edge of the mountain range as it gives way to the desert of eastern Washington. Despite it being winter, the beauty of Maple Lake is evident. The water is beautifully clear and the lake is over fifty miles long, but rather narrow. Plenty of evergreen trees dot the landscape, but nothing like the thick trees that I'm used to that hug all the roadways back in Seattle.

Riverside sits at the narrow end of the lake. From studying the map in the café, I know that the Maple River flows into the enormous Columbia River that runs through the state on its way to the Pacific Ocean. As Mom drives, I take in the view from the bridge. A maze of pathways surrounds the lake, as well as several restaurants, a golf course, and a marina, situated near the shoreline. Riverside must be a popular summer destination for people who love going in the water. Wooded hillsides and vineyards surround the valley, which, according to the welcome sign, boasts four thousand residents. The bridge takes us over the skinny leg of the otherwise massive body of water that makes up the lake. After we cross, there's a huge park and sports complex and then the high school.

She wheels into the parking lot. With it being Saturday afternoon, only a handful of cars occupy the space. My old school was massive and this one looks to be no more than a quarter of its size. It took forever to get across the campus if I had to get to a class in another building. That won't be a problem here.

There's no trash scattered around the grounds and no graffiti painted on the walls. Banners hang on the fence wishing the wrestling team luck. A fancy-looking sign in green and gold, complete with a digital display, welcomes visitors to Riverside High.

We go past her own school and pull up to grab groceries.

The lot is full of cars and I'm not in the mood to wander the aisles of the store, so as she disappears inside the supermarket, I adjust the seat and lean back to watch all the people walking by. There are lots of families coming and going and I focus on a dad with his son, who looks to be close to my age. The dad puts his arm around the kid's shoulder and says something. They both burst out laughing and a sharp pang of jealousy creeps over me.

Why couldn't I have a dad that's home, who's there when I need him? Someone to talk to when I need advice. Mom talks to kids all day and is beat when she gets home. I try not to bother her with my stuff, but if Dad was around, I could bounce things off him.

I don't remember laughing with my dad very often. Mom always seemed nervous about keeping the house immaculate and everything organized; she said his military training had made him that way and she didn't want to upset him. I think that affected her more than she realized.

I remember the one time he took me fishing last summer. I had been looking forward to spending time with Dad, and Mom packed all our favorite foods and snacks and crammed in extra blankets for our overnight camping trip. With his work so demanding and keeping him from home much of the time, it was rare that he had time for me and I was so excited that he had arranged to borrow a boat.

We listened to oldies on the radio as Dad drove to the special spot he had chosen on the Cle Elum River. We stopped at a burger place for lunch on the way and took thick chocolate shakes to go when we left. As we neared the turnoff for the river,

Dad talked more about the trout he expected we would catch. I asked him if he fished with his dad when he was growing up, but my question dampened his spirit and I wasn't sure why. He gave me a quick answer that he had learned to fish with a fellow soldier. The campsite was primitive: nestled in a dense grove of trees overlooking the wide ribbon of water that meandered through the forest.

It was mid-afternoon when we got there and Dad went about getting the fishing gear ready while I unloaded our camping supplies. He put me in charge of gathering wood for a fire, so we'd be ready for nightfall. He wanted to get in some fishing before it got dark and led the way to the water's edge. It was a gorgeous day, with the sun glinting off the river, peaceful and quiet except for the soft sound of water gurgling around rocks and the chatter of birds and squirrels. Our trip was shaping up to be great, until the actual fishing started.

I couldn't do anything right. I didn't know the names of the flies and tackle he asked me to retrieve from his box. I didn't hold the rod correctly. It was like a mission, without the joy I expected from spending time with Dad on the river. He was all business, no joking, and he implored me to take the entire thing seriously. It was stressful and he had me so nervous I couldn't even cast the line. He barked orders at me: stand like this, move your arm up a fraction, grip the line tighter—but not too tight. It was all too much and when I heard the telltale snap of the rod in my hands, my heart sank and Dad exploded.

That day is seared in my mind. I'd wanted to cry but knew he'd just get angrier. He didn't want to stay after that and we loaded everything back into the truck and headed for home. The trip home was in near silence, with Dad gripping the steering wheel so tight his knuckles were white.

As we got closer to home, Dad stopped for gas. When he got back in the truck, he turned to me and said, "I shouldn't have gotten so mad. I can get the rod repaired; it'll be fine." He moved his hand to my shoulder and I couldn't help it, I flinched. Sorrow filled his eyes and his shoulders sagged as he turned his attention to steering the truck back to the road. I turned and looked out my window, afraid my voice would betray the tears stuck in my throat. It seemed like Dad's angry outbursts were more frequent than they had been and I didn't want to be the focus of another one. I couldn't reconcile that brief glimpse of sadness I had witnessed with the anger and rage he'd exhibited at the river. That was the day I gave up trying to please him; the day I abandoned the idea of a father-son relationship; the day I lost my dad.

CHAPTER 4

We unload the groceries and while Mom prepares her stew for tonight's meal, I bring in a few more boxes from the garage. As she's sliding the dish into the oven, her cell phone rings and her smile fades. She pokes the button. "William," she says, walking from the room and down the hallway.

I strain to listen and detect a change in her inflection, which is never surprising when she talks to my dad. I catch a few words. Something about her not wanting to rehash things. I hear my name and slide across the floor in my socks to stand at the edge of the hallway. "Toby doesn't need to know the details. He has enough on his plate right now." It sounds like she's moving further into her bedroom. I can't make out anything else, just the occasional rise of her voice. What is it I don't need to know? I wonder if our financial situation is worse than I thought. I can't hear anything now. I go back to the table and pick up the list of chores she wrote out that need to be done this weekend.

I study it while I snack on a cookie—get the grill, a housewarming gift from Mom's realtor, set up outside, unpack some boxes, hook up our tiny televisions, the second-hand computer, and wireless stuff, a note about school lunches—but I can't get Mom's words out of my head. *Doesn't need to know?*

Mom returns, blotting at her eyes. She should be stronger now that they're not together and she doesn't have to deal with him all the time. Maybe it's too many years of being mistreated and barked at by him. She occupies herself by rearranging a cabinet while I contemplate the chores. I can tell she doesn't want to talk about the phone call and pretend I don't notice the evidence of tears.

"Can I just take money for lunch?" I close my eyes and pray she agrees. A new kid carrying a sack lunch is an invitation for a problem. I don't want to be that kid. I'll toss Mom's lunch in the trash if it comes to it. Maybe I need to find a job—

"This week, yes," she says, cutting my thought short. "We've got to clamp down on spending until I get a handle on our expenses here. Let's see how it goes."

I breathe out relief. A one-week reprieve is better than nothing. Mom dries the cutting board and slips it into a drawer and moves to the living area. She starts unpacking boxes, and I notice it's getting chillier. The house has a pellet stove and it's another item on our to-do list. A local supplier had delivered two pallets of the heavy bags of wood pellets and put them next to the driveway. With it being February, there's still enough winter to come and Mom got a deal if she bought them in bulk.

I find the instructions taped to the front of the stove and I give them a quick scan.

I muscle in a bag of pellets and load the hopper before I flip the switch to the on position. A soft purr signals it's working and a few minutes later I watch the pellets drop and a flame glow through the window.

Mom wants her books unpacked and put on the bookshelves. She could open her own library with this massive collection. She spends the bulk of her summer vacation reading fiction. I remember she likes them arranged by author, as I pile in her collection of Agatha Christie books and leave ample space between them and her Louise Penny novels. I can't believe the thickness of the books by Diana Gabaldon. They have to be over two inches each. It would take me a lifetime to read just one of them. It doesn't take long to empty the containers and I cart them to the garage.

We've made quite a dent in the boxes, so I move the remaining unpacked cartons into a neat row along one side of the space, leaving enough room for the van. Mom doesn't need the hassle of scraping windows or dealing with snow in the mornings.

While I'm breaking down the cardboard, my mind wanders to Monday and my first day at Riverside High. I'm dreading it. Mom thinks I'll make friends and find some silly club to join, but I'm not holding out much hope for that. I can't imagine I'm going to have anything in common with people like Molly and Ginny, who've lived in this tiny town all their lives. I'll be lucky to slog through it without dying of boredom.

Mom paints this town with an optimistic brush, like it's the answer to all our problems. I'm not convinced it will solve everything. We may have escaped Dad, but his anger follows us everywhere; it's made Mom quiet and lonely. She's lost her confidence and I've never seen her so vulnerable. I hope it's temporary and she finds what she hopes is here. What if she's even more stressed here? What if this place doesn't work?

I've told myself I have to do better and I sure don't want to embarrass Mom. Not in a place like this where everyone will know everything that happens. I want to do the right thing, and I don't want to let her down. I'm just afraid I'll do something I'll regret again. Sometimes I feel out of control and even though I know I should handle things differently, I can't stop myself in time. I'm going to try harder than I ever have, so Mom has one less thing to worry about here.

I haven't had time to wrap my head around all of these changes. It seems like from the time Mom said she got the job and we were leaving the city, that everything has been moving at warp speed. Mom and Dad have had their ups and downs, but I got the impression Mom wasn't looking for a divorce when I spied on them from the top of the stairs. I'm still not sure what happened to go from the idea of us staying in Seattle while Dad went to his new post to them getting divorced and Mom and I on our own in this place.

As frustrated as Dad makes me, I do worry about him, especially now that he's all alone. He'll probably just volunteer to work more, now that he has no reason to come home.

Our family wasn't perfect and I know things could have been better, but it was all we had. Now, we're stuck here, no matter what. Mom made her choice and I know she thinks it's the right one, but it seems like she jumped at the first opportunity and this was it. I wonder if she could have found something better closer to Seattle.

There's a small hot water heater and the cheap brand of furnace installed in the closet in the garage. They match the tacky plastic molding and baseboards throughout the place. I know she's excited to have a new house, but I can tell this is a bare bones model. All the cheap finishes look okay now, but I doubt things will last much past the warranty period. I wish she would have asked me to look at it with her and I could have seen this place before today.

Maybe, if I had come with her, we could have found a better place, a house with more room, if she trusted me more.

With some of the boxes gone and the rest organized, there's room to stack the pellets inside. I grab a pair of work gloves and start moving the heavy bags to a spot near the door leading into the house. As I tote each bag and stack it, I realize there's no way Mom could manage carrying these and I'll need to make sure I keep the hopper filled.

It takes me the rest of the afternoon to make the hundred trips back and forth and the muscles in my shoulders and back are protesting. The whole time I work, only one car drives by on our street. I guess I shouldn't be surprised, since we're in the middle of nowhere.

I use the money Mom left on the counter and pick up a propane tank for the new grill at the local hardware store.

The clerks in the store are just as friendly as Molly, and everyone I run into smiles and says something in the way of a greeting. The last few weeks all I've had are people smiling at me, offering advice, from Dr. Hawes, the therapists I had to see, to the counselor at school.

"What do you think of your new school?" Mom asks, coming outside as I'm working on the grill.

"It looks okay," I say, taking a break to rest on the patio, wiping grease from the tank on my jeans. "I'm not looking forward to being the new kid again. It's no fun having everyone look at you."

Concern clouds her eyes. "I know it's not what we planned, Toby. I'm sorry."

I make some adjustments with a little wrench supplied in the package of instructions. "It's not your fault, Mom. I'll be fine. It's not like I haven't done it before. I just want that first day to be over, so I can blend in and not be on display."

"I promise you, it's the last time. You'll be able to finish high school here."

I have my doubts but hope this is a promise she can keep. "Do you ever wish you had more than me? Another kid, I mean."

She sighs and shrugs, looking across to the hills. "Oh, there are times I think it would have been fun to have a houseful of kids, but with your dad deployed and gone so much, I think it would have been difficult. What about you? Do you wish you had a brother or sister?"

"Sometimes." I shrug. "I think it would be fun to have someone to hang out with…"

She nods sadly and turns to me. "I can see that. My sister and I had such a strong bond growing up, even though we aren't close now with her so far away. Sometimes we'd bicker and fight with each other like you couldn't imagine, but she wouldn't hear of anyone else picking on me."

Mom wipes her eyes with the dust rag she's holding and her voice thickens. "I worry that you haven't got to experience much of the fun of being a child. Because it's been you and me so much of the time on our own, I sometimes burden you with too many adult problems and rely on you more than I should. I think you've missed out on the innocence of being a kid. Your dad's job doesn't help with us having to move all the time. It makes it hard to maintain close friendships or even have the chance to do things with kids your own age."

She sighs and says, "I know you haven't had much luck with friends before…"

I wrap her in a hug and feel the soft sobs she's trying to suppress cascade through her body. "Don't be sad, Mom. We're going to be okay here. You did the right thing." I'm not sure I believe what I'm telling her, but can't bear seeing her so distraught. Mom's shoulders droop and you can see the exhaustion in her thin frame; it's been years since her clothes fit her properly. It's almost monthly she sits down to take them in, an inch here or there.

"I know starting over at a new school isn't going to be easy," she continues and I know where this is going. Does she even see me when she gives me these lectures, or does she feel like she's in class, helping another woman's son? "And while it's not what I wanted for you, in my heart I believe it's for the best. It will give you a chance to leave our past behind you. It's your opportunity to buckle down and prove to me and, more importantly, to yourself, that you can succeed in school."

She offers me an encouraging smile. "You're smart and kind-hearted, Toby. I see it. You just need to do a better job of making good choices." Her tone hardens slightly and she's not looking at me anymore. "I want your homework done when you get home. I don't want to have to argue with you or treat you like you're in elementary school. I expect you to come home and get your work done. Then when I get home," her eyes look back to me, "maybe we can have a life, watch some movies, go explore Riverside, do something other than work. I want our home to be peaceful, a refuge, a place we'll be happy." She gestures to the wall behind her. "I promise we won't leave. We've got this brand-new house and I expect you to listen to what the therapist told you. I don't want holes from your fists in these walls or broken doors from you throwing things or slamming them. Do you think you can do that?"

I give her a nod but she just doesn't understand. I've never wanted to react to Dad, to act the way I did, but I've never been able to stop myself. My mom has a calmness, a softness, like this place, this town, that I just don't have. When I want to defend her, when I want to defend myself, there's an anger that rises inside of me—an adrenaline rush, the therapist called it. I'm embarrassed about the things I've done in the past, but I don't know how to fix it. I don't know if it's why Dad has left. If it's why he reacts the way he does, too.

Mom goes back inside and I gather my tools and stare out at the darkness, wishing a fresh start was as easy as moving.

CHAPTER 5

Now

The first time I saw him, he was outside of his house in the late afternoon, as dusk settled into the valley. The sumptuous aroma of bread and the sweet smell of fresh apple pie was heavy in the air. I'd been exploring the neighborhood, looking for leftovers, as I'd been avoiding going downtown in the alleys behind the shops and restaurants. There was always something in the dumpsters, but a few shop owners had shooed me away. I usually spent my time in the fields and orchards, but during the winter, there was little to eat, with all the errant fruit long gone from the farms and the fields bare. I had resorted to roaming through blocks of houses, letting my nose guide me.

I sniffed the air and caught whiffs of the neighborhood. The scents of people, cars, someone's outdoor grill that still had bits of meat stuck on it, dogs, and cats filtered through my nostrils. It smelled like a home.

From some bushes in front of an unoccupied house across the street, I watched the boy, not yet a man, tote heavy bags inside the garage. He made trip after trip and slouched with far more than the weight of the bags on his shoulders. His brow furrowed in thought as he'd pluck a bag from the pallet and heave it on his shoulder, before depositing it on the stack inside.

A few times, he muttered to himself as he toiled. I was drawn to him and hunkered down to watch. He took great care to flatten the boxes and pile the cardboard before he made neat stacks with the heavy bags. When he was done, he examined the space and adjusted the piles until they were straight and tidy. I could never have spent so long straightening them.

I knew it was his first night there. Several times he stopped and looked up and down the street, bending and stretching his back. I thought maybe he saw me, but he never even glanced my way. I sensed worry in him, but what did he have to be concerned about?

After he shut the garage door, my curiosity piqued, I crept closer to the house and gave the front perimeter a good sniff. I couldn't detect any animal smells, save for the deer and squirrels that had made tracks through the property.

I did, however, identify the irresistible and savory scent of beef and rich gravy, and my stomach growled so loudly I was sure they could hear me. Dinner—I'd forgotten. There was a house at the end of the street I hadn't yet checked, and the children who lived there had a habit of leaving remnants of their snacks on the driveway.

Before I left, I took one last peek through the window and saw a hint of a flame burning in one of those fancy stoves and I longed for a house like this one. A real home, where I could curl up by the fire.

CHAPTER 6

Then

The crisp morning air hurries my steps across town to school. The frost on the trees and fenceposts along my way reflect the morning sun like those fancy Christmas cards. The faint babble of the narrow stream that runs along the fields and orchards keeps me company until I get to downtown.

I spent most of the night not sleeping, thinking about how to keep calm today, and Mom's advice echoes even now, as I cross the bridge over the lake and make my way toward the school, passing by the sports complex and down the sidewalk to the main entrance. I don't normally get nervous, it's been years since I've really worried about what people think about me, but with Mom's words going over in my mind, I see everyone checking me out, glancing at me, and whispering when I pass by them. I feel eyes staring at me as I reach for the door.

The lady in the office is friendly and has everything ready for me and she assigns a student to show me around and get me to my first class.

Lyle's a tall guy, clean-cut, with dark hair. I'm surprised when he gives me a sincere smile, his teeth straight, except for a tiny gap between the front two. Guys like Lyle at my old school never had time for me, too confident, too sure, too many friends already. They were too wrapped up with their jock friends to notice me and were only nice when teachers were watching. He is so polite and warm when he introduces himself and offers to show me around the campus, I'm sure it's for the benefit of the staff in the office.

As he chats with me on our walk through the hallways, I begin to second-guess my rush to judgment. He's friendly and barely drops his smile for a moment. First, he takes me through the hallway and makes sure my locker combo works. His hands have a few cuts and old scars on them. Working hands. Hands that suggest there is more to Lyle than his pretty-boy looks. Maybe I'd been too quick to judge him.

"You're lucky, you have a top locker. Mine's on the bottom and I always hit my head on the one above it," he says, laughing, putting his hand on the top of his head and rubbing it.

He leads the way through the hall, saying hello to each of the students that he passes.

"I guess you know everyone, huh?" I ask.

He laughs and grins. "I never thought of it, but yeah, I probably do." As we travel through the hallway, he talks about living in Riverside all his life, as have many of his friends. His great-grandparents settled here and started farming almost a hundred years ago, which is completely mad, and his entire family has lived here for generations. I've never known anyone with real roots in one place. His parents run the same farm, although it has been modernized over the years. I don't know anyone who lives on a farm, or is enthusiastic about it, but I imagine that comes with expectations too. Is there a hint of reluctance I hear when he talks about his family and their presumption that he'll take over the farm?

He gives me an overview of the classrooms organized in wings by subjects and walks me to each of my classroom doors in the main building. "So, you came from Seattle? I've only been there a few times. I guess you're used to a much bigger school." His eyes glint with a hint of excitement.

I nod. I don't particularly want to tell him my life story. "Yeah, it was huge," I say, wrestling with what else is interesting but tells him nothing about *me*. "Over three thousand students. It was super crowded and hectic during class changes."

"Wow, I can't imagine that many kids. I bet the lunchroom was out of control."

"We had three different lunch periods and I'd usually grab something at one of the food trucks that showed up each day," I reply, remembering those cheesy tacos I ate three times a week. The ones I'd eat on my own. It seemed like just when I started to find a group and gain acceptance, we moved to a new town. I'd had my hopes pinned on making Seattle my last move.

"That would be cool," says Lyle, pointing to another one of my classrooms. "One of my mom's friends is the cook here, though her cooking is nothing like what you're used to, I'm sure. We have one food truck in town and it's only active during picking season. It's a taco truck." He grimaces and adds, "It travels the country roads and goes around to all the orchards and is popular with the seasonal workers."

"Not a fan of Mexican food?"

He shakes his head. "There's an overabundance of it around here and it's not my first choice. We could use a new restaurant or two."

A couple of girls walk by and say hello to Lyle. He calls them by name and says he'll meet up with them in class next period. He gives me a huge grin.

Lyle leads me through a door in the back that connects to another building. "This is the lunchroom, library, gym, and most of our vocational classes."

He studies my schedule. "We have gym class together this afternoon. We've also got baseball tryouts after school tomorrow. You should come," he says, studying me.

"Um, I'm not too sure," I reply. I've never played on a team, just in gym class, and I can't imagine I would make the team even if I gave it a shot. I don't want to embarrass myself on day one, or promise to be involved with something I'll only have to give up.

"Coach Hobson isn't bad either. You've got him for English too. You'll like him. We've got a great bunch of guys on the team. We're doing a quick practice at lunch today."

I bob my head, without committing one way or the other. Lyle continues our tour, pointing out my classrooms. "I'm in your math class right before lunch. I'll catch up with you there. Maybe we can grab lunch before practice?" he suggests, greeting another boy and walking toward the office.

"Sounds good. I'll see you there," I say as I open the door to my first period Spanish class.

Despite thinking of Cal and the other guys at my old school as friends, most days I wasn't with them. I chose them because I didn't really fit anywhere else. Truth is, I'm not sure I fit in with them either. They would have devoured a kid like Lyle. They would have sneered at him and made fun of him for his perfectly ironed plaid shirt and jeans.

*

The morning chugs along; a familiar routine, but full of friendly faces and small-town chatter. Lyle finds me in the lunchroom and after we grab sandwiches, with him leading, we pass by the gym, to the baseball field, a fair distance from and behind the track that surrounds the football field.

Coach Hobson remembers me from class and welcomes me to the practice session. It's hard for me to reconcile my English teacher—in a sports coat and dress pants, with perfect penmanship, who discussed the love story in *A Farewell to Arms* this morning with more feeling than I could have imagined—with the man standing before me now in his green and gold sweats adorned with the large head of a goat. His voice is loud and firm and he calls the boys by name and tells them to form up in various spots for batting, catching, and running. He takes me by the shoulder and guides me to the pitching area.

Nobody else is there, just him. He gives me a glove and tosses me the ball. "Go ahead and throw me a few," he says, crouching down in a catcher's position.

I look around, thankful none of the others are watching. I've not attempted any sports since fishing with Dad. If I didn't do it, I couldn't make a mistake and be told how inept I am, but here I am now, not knowing what I'm doing. I throw the first ball. He gives me some advice on how to place my feet and where my elbow and shoulder should be and I try it a few more times.

"Great job, Toby." Coach Hobson continues to tweak my stance and demonstrates a few pitches, pointing out where I need to change. He explains how to start with the weight on my back leg. With exaggerated motions, he demonstrates how to lift my front leg but maintain my balance. He shows me and guides me, stressing the importance of releasing the ball with my elbow above my shoulder, which decreases the chance of an arm injury.

I send a few more balls his way and he smiles each time the ball smacks against his well-worn glove. "That's it, perfect." I keep throwing, remembering the mechanics he showed me, and his words of praise warm something inside me.

Coach Hobson whistles to round up the rest of the players around me. "Great job, guys. Remember, last day of tryouts is tomorrow and we've just got a few more spots to fill."

I watch the guys, all of whom are joking and laughing with each other, gather the equipment and head toward the gym, when Coach Hobson grabs my shoulder. "Toby, I hope you'll come tomorrow. You've got quite the arm. I'd like to see you play."

I shrug, not wanting to commit, and he follows my gaze to the group of players making their way to the gym. "They're a good group of young men. Real team players who support each other on and off the field." He releases his grip on my shoulder and nods at me. "I think you'd find some good friends in the group. You could give it a whirl and if you decide it's not for you, there won't be any hard feelings."

I enjoy being around the other guys, doing something physical. Their encouraging eyes and easy-going attitudes helped me relax and nobody judged me when I needed some direction. It's not at all what I expected. Coach Hobson makes me feel like part of the group, not like a new kid. He's not focused on my past and where I lived, just on how I could be a part of the team. His guidance is easy to follow and his corrections are never harsh. He treats me like all the other guys and doesn't draw attention to my inexperience. That sort of enthusiasm is pretty hard to resist. "I'll be there, thanks for the help today." I hurry to get back to the main building and catch up with Lyle.

"What did you think?" Lyle asks as we rush through the door.

"I've never had an English teacher who could swing a bat like that!" We laugh. "He wants me to come tomorrow night."

Lyle's smile widens. "That's great news. He wouldn't say that unless you were good."

We grab our books and go our separate ways to class.

"You're the new kid?"

The afternoon flies by in a blur, and before I know it, it's time to head home. I take off in the direction of the street, but somebody stops me, flashes a grin my way.

A tall guy with perfect hair, his shoulders back, chest puffed out. He's leaning on a fence, smoking while he and his buddy chat with a couple of girls. They're on the edge of the school grounds, the low white fence they lean against, serving as the barrier between the parking lot and the adjacent property. The grass in front of the fence is well worn and patchy from the constant foot traffic.

He lifts his chin at me in a greeting.

I nod and take a few steps closer. The gleam in his eye and the five o'clock shadow along his cheeks and chin make him look older, like he should work here instead of attending. His tall, almost proud posture, the worn leather jacket, the way his eyes seem to take in everything around him, the ownership of what is clearly his space. He herds the girls away with a flick of his eyes as I approach. As he watches them walk away, the corners of his mouth curve into a satisfying smile.

"I'm Evan and this is Jerry." He gestures to his friend and then turns back to me. "You're in my English class." Jerry, a short, stocky guy, with a tattoo on the inside of his wrist, gives a slight dip of his head, but says nothing, deferring to Evan.

I picture the classroom and have a vague memory of the guy with wavy dark hair in the back row. "Right, I saw you there today. I'm Toby." I start to walk away and continue to the street.

"You're from Seattle, right?" Evan continues, rushing ahead of me to walk backwards. He's directly in my way, and I'm sure he means to be. Everything is slow and deliberate, in the way he moves, in what he says—as though this is a conversation he has with all the new kids.

"Yeah, we just moved here a few days ago," I reply, and stand still.

"I saw Lyle showing you around. Looks like he got you an audition with the baseball team?"

"I thought I'd try it."

Evan snickers. "If you're on the team, the teachers will love you," he says, glancing at Jerry with a playful smirk. "Us, not so much." They both laugh.

"This town will be way too small for you, Emerald City. There's almost nothing to do. We know some of the best places to escape the village though." He flashes me a knowing grin. "You're welcome to join us," he says as he juts his chin in my direction as a farewell.

Evan looks like the type of guy Mom would warn me to avoid. Like the type of guy she worries I am and doesn't want me to be. He strikes me as powerful, as he regains his perch against the fence. He pays no attention to the other students, keeping his eyes on me.

Why would he reach out to me?

Mom doesn't want me to repeat my past mistakes. Her words have been playing in my head and I rub my bottom lip as I keep walking. I know Mom doesn't want me falling in with a bad crowd, but the chances of Evan being a bad guy are pretty slim. In a small school like this, they'd be all over him if he was real trouble. I think Riverside's idea of a juvenile delinquent and Seattle's idea are two very different things. I'll talk more to Evan tomorrow and see.

Evan is probably just tired of being looked at like a second-class citizen if he's not playing sports like the other guys. That's how I was treated anyway.

Lyle doesn't seem like he's like that, or the rest of the guys on the team. But being friends with kids like Lyle invites more problems: good kids want to know where you're from, their parents want to know who your parents are, that their perfect sons aren't hanging around with troubled guys, guys with anger problems, guys who don't know how to control their emotions, families with secrets.

CHAPTER 7

I clear the bridge and make my way to the country road that will take me home, approaching the corner with the huge tree. My first day was different than I expected. This town fits Lyle like a well-worn shoe, but I get the impression Evan's restless. I'm certain he doesn't share the idea that Riverside is the rural paradise the locals make it out to be. While Evan is itching for something more, Lyle comes across as resigned, if not content, to his life and the traditions of his family in this little valley. My cell phone rings and I dig it from my pocket to look at the display.

Dad's name pops on the screen, and my finger hovers over the green button and then the red one. I haven't heard from him since he walked out that day. After what has to be the fifth ring, I punch the green button, hoping for the best.

"Hey, Dad."

"Guess what I just got in the mail?" Classic Dad, barking at me without taking a breath. Every conversation we have is more like a speech.

My shoulders tense and I can visualize my dad's narrowed brows, his eyes staring at me. "Uh, I don't know," I reply.

"Just a nice little follow-up letter from the folks down at juvenile justice. Seems you and your mother forgot to mention your little foray into the city and your subsequent arrest." His tone is full of annoyance.

"I wasn't really arrested."

"Don't try to split hairs with me, Toby." He sighs and his voice softens as he says, "This kind of behavior worries me. I know you've been having a hard time, but this is unexpected. What's going on with you? Do you want to talk about it?"

I'm not in the mood to rehash old news. I've done enough talking about it with Mom and all the counselors. "It was wrong. I've got it under control."

With a weary breath, he says, "Trust me, you can think you have things under control and then suddenly they're not. Are you sure you're doing okay?" Dad sounds exhausted.

"It's fine. There isn't going to be any more trouble. Not in this place, there's nowhere to go."

"You're lucky you're not living under my roof any longer. This type of behavior is beyond disappointing and such an embarrassment. You need to shape up, Toby. Had I known about this, I would have made sure you spent some time locked up for your fight with me. I can't believe your mother didn't tell me. I'm going to give her a piece of my mind. It's no wonder you're failing classes and skipping school. She obviously doesn't have any control over you."

Fury bubbles up in my throat. Mom is not weak. She works herself into the ground to take care of everything. Where has he been? You can't ignore us half of the time and then try to tell us how to live. "It's clear you don't care about either one of us." I hit the button to disconnect the call in an effort to diffuse the rage I'm feeling. The therapist said to remove myself from a conversation that provokes anger and wait—but I think I'll need more than fifteen minutes.

I make the turn at the bigleaf maple and anger swells up inside me, just like it always does. My hands are shaking and the sting of angry tears burns my throat. I stare ahead and practice some of the breathing exercises that sometimes help. I concentrate on the blue sky above the towering tree and let out a long breath. I try to slow the pounding of my heart, but the quiet is interrupted by a rustle in the grass along the edge of the road.

I strain to look in the overgrowth, stand still and listen again, but I don't see or hear anything. I put my phone back in my pocket, when a flash of golden fur catches my eye. Out from the grassy brush slinks a dog. The movement startles me, and my heart hammers slightly, still affected by the anger I'd only just managed to contain, as I take a deep breath and move for a closer look at him. He has a generous jaw, and soft wide ears, along with the deep chest—a golden retriever?

His gentle brown eyes lock onto mine. He doesn't have a collar and his fur is matted and dirty—streaks of thick brown mud run up the bottoms of his legs, adorning his paws, and the rest of him has darkened slightly—is he golden or is he a lighter blonde? It's impossible to tell. I bend down to him. He doesn't flinch or move away from me as we stare at each other, and I can feel his breath on my cheek.

His face is the only surface not covered in dirt or mud. His dark eyes and blackish-brown nose are in perfect contrast with his golden face. I put a hand on top of his head and he closes his eyes as I pet him. His eyelashes are long and several shades darker than the fur on his face. I make a move to stand and he opens his eyes, looking straight into mine, the deep brown orbs full of warmth and compassion. I start to pick up my bag. Somebody's missing him. "Go on home, boy," I say, gesturing with my hand to shoo him away.

His sweet eyes remind me of the puppy I fell in love with when I was in elementary school. Somebody Mom knew from work had a golden retriever who had puppies. All three of us had gone to visit them a few times and spent time playing with them on the grass, letting them romp and run all over us. I was desperate to have one. I picked out a male, who always ran to me first, and Mom and Dad decided I was old enough to have the responsibility. It was the beginning of summer, so I'd have three months to spend with him and train him. He was gorgeous and cuddly and his fur shimmered in the sunlight. I was so excited, but none of us knew how much things would soon change. That we'd never get to bring the puppy home. That our lives would get so much more complicated.

The dog backs up a step, but then moves toward me. I take a few steps down the road and he maintains a distance, but follows, flopping down his giant paws like it's taking all the effort in the world. I turn and walk back to him. His eyes won't leave mine. They tug at my heart. I glance down his narrow back and notice his fur has a natural wave that travels down it.

He's so thin. His ribs are sticking out and there isn't an ounce of fat on him. He must be lost. I wonder where he lives and how far he's traveled or if anyone is looking for him. He hasn't been fed. He looks like he hasn't been looked after by anyone for a long time.

The dog sits and holds up a paw, dangling it in the air with an expectant face. I can't help but laugh at his greeting and hope flashes in his dark eyes. His mouth is open slightly and his dark lips form a wide smile that spans across his jaws. Despite his bedraggled appearance, he looks happy.

"Go home," I say, with less insistence than last time, but he makes no move to leave. I'm not sure how Mom would react to me bringing home a stray dog. She doesn't really need another mouth to feed right now. I take a few more steps down the road toward home and look back to find him following me. He's limping with his front leg, the same one he lifted, and I slow my pace.

Each time I turn around, the dog's soulful eyes bore into mine. With each gaze, it's like he's pleading for help. I slow some more and pat my leg, urging the dog to come closer. He complies and I take a look at his leg. I don't see any injuries, but with all the mud, it's hard to tell. He stays by my side as we trek down the road. If I stop or slow my pace, he does the same.

He may be filthy and grubby but he walks tall and proud. He has a prance to his gait, like a horse trotting in a parade. His coat may be shaggy but every step he takes is with certainty—like he was waiting for me and now he knows where he's going. But dogs don't think like that, right?

Since he's limping, we take the road with slow steps. Despite it being winter, it's sunny and feels warmer than the forty-five degrees displayed on my phone when I checked it when I got up this morning. The fields and orchards are quiet and bare, resting for the season. It's just under a mile to our house and I keep telling the dog we're almost there, and each time he looks at me, but doesn't seem phased by the length of our walk. His pace is slow and steady, his tail swinging from side to side.

Outside of my limited experience with the puppy, I don't know much about dogs, only what I've noticed from friends who've had them. In middle school, we had a neighbor with some sort of basset hound mix, and that dog loved to run around the neighborhood and sometimes he'd howl for hours at night. All the dogs I've met seem to love to run and they're always hungry, willing to do any trick for a bite of a tasty biscuit. Just the other day, I laughed at a post I saw online showing photos of dogs and their owners who look alike. The little old lady with curly white hair and tiny eyes that looks like her powder puff of a Bichon Frise and the guy with the long flowing hair that resembles his Afghan hound are so funny. I study the golden retriever before me and realize we don't look anything alike, except we both have brown eyes.

I watch his nose wiggle as he lifts his head higher and takes in the scents from the breeze. I don't smell anything, but I'm sure he can detect the subtlest odors from the fruit orchards and grassy fields we pass by on our way home. He's focused on sniffing the air—maybe it's new territory for him.

I tell him about our new house and he looks at me, as if he is listening. My phone chimes and I dig it out, hoping it's not Dad again, but instead, I find a text from Mom. She's checking in to make sure I'm home, reminding me she'll be here within the hour. Sometimes I wonder if she realizes I'm sixteen. I look at the dog and slide the phone back into my pocket. "Moms, huh?" The dog turns his gentle eyes on me and as we turn on our street, I realize how comforting it feels to have him next to me.

When I get home, I open the garage door and coax the dog inside. He doesn't hesitate to follow me even though he has no idea he can trust me. Dogs can recognize seizures and all sorts of medical problems even before they occur; maybe they can recognize danger the same way. I search the boxes and find the one with the spare linens and open the tape and pull out several old blankets and towels. After folding them to form a makeshift bed, I point to it. "Come on, boy, you can rest here, so you won't be on the cold concrete." The dog moves to the blanket and lies down.

I take a look at his paws and legs. The pads are worn and rough, several of them torn, and I probe along the front leg that seems to be bothering him. He lets me move the leg and touch it, without flinching or making a move to push me away with his snout. He's content to lie there and let me do my examination. Complete trust. He's already decided I'm no threat. I have no idea what I'm doing, but try to compare it to the other leg. They feel the same and the dog doesn't jerk away when I touch it.

His thick nails are torn and a mess, not to mention the huge mass of tangles on his backside. His sturdy paws are overgrown with fur and mud-covered tufts. I pat his head and he exhales a long sigh. "I'll go get you some water and something to eat. Wait here."

The dog's brows rise and he watches as I go through the door to the house. I rummage in the refrigerator and find some leftover chicken from last night's dinner. As I'm chopping it up, I wonder what I'll do with him—Dad would never allow an animal in the house, but he's not here to forbid it.

I finish the chicken and add a few bits of cheese to it before I find one of Mom's stainless-steel mixing bowls and begin filling it with water as Mom walks into the kitchen, flinging her bag down on one of the kitchen counters and leaning on the counter with a satisfied smile.

"How did your first day go?" she asks.

"Not bad," I say, wondering just how much to tell her. "I've already signed up for baseball. The coach wants me to come to the last day of tryouts tomorrow. Those ladies at the café weren't kidding when they mentioned the passion for sports around here." I pause. "Dad called." I take a deep breath. "He got some sort of notice from the juvenile authorities and wanted to yell at me about it, I guess. He sounded so tired…"

Mom's eyes fall to the cuff of her sweater and she picks at a stray piece of yarn. "I know his words can be hurtful, but he doesn't mean it. Try not to blame him for everything. There are things you don't understand." She shuts her eyes and clenches her teeth. Even mentioning him makes her feel uneasy. She fills a mug with water for tea. "Tell me more about this baseball idea."

"I don't know much yet."

Her eyes flash with interest. "It sounds exciting," she says, but I can already see the logical side of her brain taking over, and she pauses. "But you've never played sports." I love Mom but she doesn't have to take the fun out of everything. "They take up so much time and I don't want you to get distracted from your schoolwork—repeating last year… you've got to make your studies a priority."

"Coach Hobson told us the same thing. Apparently, he won't tolerate anything less than a B on our report cards."

"Hmm," she says, slipping off her coat. "Well, I do love the idea of you having something fun to do. It just can't interfere with your classes." She frowns at the bowls on the counter.

"What are you doing with all this?"

I gesture to her, carrying the water and handing her the food bowl. As we step down into the garage, the dog opens his eyes to follow us. I set the bowl down near him and he leaps to his feet, nose high in the air. His eyes are on Mom and the food she's delivering. After a polite sip from the water bowl, he moves his nose to Mom and the chicken in her hand. He sits at her feet and lifts his snout high in the air, inching closer to the bowl. She bends and places the food next to his water and he devours the chicken in a few bites and then licks the bowl until it shines, lifting his head only as if to say thanks, every few seconds.

"Toby, where did you find this poor guy?" Her face lights up as she gives him a gentle pet on the head, but her eyes linger over his muddy legs, already taking into account the towels he's lying on, that she'll need to wash.

"On the way home from school. He followed me," I say, trying to paint his appearance in as positive a light as possible. I gesture with my eyes and add, "I'm worried about his front leg. He was limping all the way here. I felt it, but I can't tell what could be wrong."

Mom looks at her watch and bends down to examine the dog's leg. "I think we'd better get it checked out right away." She sighs and moves her eyes toward the garage door. "Load him in the back of the van and I'll make a call." She flutters her hands at me.

CHAPTER 8

Now

I remember that first day when I followed my boy home. Karen called him Toby. I liked the sound of it—strong, but friendly. I saw the concern in her eyes when Toby told her about my limp. With great care, he picked me up and put me in the back of their van, making sure I had a blanket. I stood and looked out the window, watching as he climbed into the rear seat and Karen ran from the house and jumped behind the wheel, accelerating down the road. I had to steady myself when she punched the gas pedal, to keep from falling against the door.

She told Toby the vet didn't have any openings, but suggested the animal shelter. I shuddered, remembering the stories from some of my friends about shelters and none of them made me want to visit one. Fear pulsed through me and I began to pant.

Toby reached his arm over the back of the seat and stroked my head and neck. "Don't worry, you're going to be okay." His words soothed me and when I looked in his eyes, all I saw was love. It was the same sensation I had when I met him that afternoon on the road.

I was wary and fearful to come out from the protection of the tall grass and bushes, but when I saw Toby, I knew I'd be safe with him. I'd watched him, after all. I trusted he wouldn't hurt me, and that trust never wavered in all the years we spent together.

Approaching him that day was the best decision I ever made. When Toby bent down and talked to me, I could sense the goodness in his heart. I relished the warmth and gentleness he delivered with each stroke on my head. I wanted him to be my person. I wanted to be his dog.

But it wasn't just goodness I sensed in Toby that day.

Toby changed in the years we spent together, but when we met, he was lost, he was just a boy. There was anger and disappointment in him, a sadness that radiated from his body, and I felt like he needed me just as much as I needed him. They say people are made for each other, that there are soulmates in this world, two people destined for one another, and this was me and Toby.

When he tried to shoo me away, I could tell he didn't mean it. He had a kind heart and I knew he was hurting. He was hesitant, at first, but when I held up my paw, he smiled and I loved it. Beneath the sadness in his eyes, I saw a glimmer of hope. He was too young to be so sad, so angry. His distress was evident and I knew I could relieve some of it.

Despite Toby's attempt to send me away, I knew deep inside he needed someone to talk to, a friend, a companion. It had been a long time since I'd had a person and I'd been searching for the right one.

I started to walk and favored my front leg, limping a little.

When he patted his leg and slowed down so I could catch up to him, I knew we'd be together forever. He petted me and scratched my ears and didn't seem to mind the mud. On that walk to Toby's house, I forgot the many days it had been since I'd eaten a real meal. I was so excited to have found my person, I wanted to jump on him and lick him in the face, but I resisted. Sometimes humans don't like that. I knew I needed to be on my best behavior and show him I would always be by his side. I matched his steps and stayed right next to him, even when I detected the scent of fresh manure in the field we passed.

When Toby petted my ears and stroked my head, I could feel the tension in him dissipate.

I already loved him.

I never knew my father, but throughout the years had learned that some fathers could be cruel. I hoped his wasn't. I'll never forget my mother—her sweet smell and the softness of her body. She was warm and tender, although she'd give me a good nibble on the neck if I got too rough. She took care of all of our needs and I still remember how much I loved it when she'd lick me with her warm tongue. Those early days where all I did was snuggle in a pile with my brothers and sisters, huddled close to my mother, were wonderful. It's the safest I've ever felt.

After spending those first weeks in the house, we got to go outside and we had so much fun chasing each other in the soft grass, exploring so many new scents and chewing on everything we encountered. Lots of humans came to visit us and hold us. I enjoyed all the attention and loved snuggling against them, listening to their voices, and smelling them. As we got older, more people came and took one of my sisters. I was so sad that first night without her, but Mom explained we couldn't stay with her forever.

It was such a sinking feeling and my first lesson about life. I loved my mother more than anything and couldn't imagine ever leaving her. She was my whole world. When I watch Toby and his mom, I sense their strong bond: his love for her is unwavering. I saw it in the way she looked in the review mirror that day, to check on us, and in her kind smile when she saw Toby comforting me. They were a team.

As my siblings and I grew, I remember a family with a young boy who came to visit several times. The boy was my favorite of all the people who held me. I hoped he would be the one to take me home, but it turned out I went to live with a young couple instead. I longed for my mother in those early days and I often wonder what happened to all my brothers and sisters. I craved the comfort of a family.

I looked out the window at the shops lining the main street. We drove through town and within minutes the van stopped outside a large building. Toby carried me up the ramp and through the glass doors. He held me against him while his mom spoke to a young man at the counter. The desperate whines and whimpers of animals emanating from behind a large door beyond the front desk made the hair on my back stand on end. I didn't want to be there and squirmed in Toby's arms.

A few minutes later, a woman with a kind face, named Trish, wearing scrubs with dogs and cats on them, ushered us into a smaller room. Toby set me on a narrow, padded counter that connected to the wall. I felt my legs shake, and Toby ran his hand over my back. As he massaged my ears, I tried to relax.

The space was set up like an examination room at the vet's office. I've only been to the vet's office a few times, and except for the soft treats they gave me, I never liked going there much. The unpleasant odors of antiseptics and isopropyl alcohol stung my nose and reminded me of those past visits.

The woman examined my mouth and ears, listened to my heart and lungs, and ruffled my ears when she was done.

She grinned at me and then turned to Toby and Karen. "He's healthy, outside of being underweight and needing a bit of grooming. My advice is to keep your eye on the leg and if you notice it again, get him to the vet for an X-ray. That's the only definitive test that could rule out a hairline fracture or something like that."

Relief spread over Toby's face and his shoulders relaxed.

He ran his hands over me and smiled, telling me everything was okay. With each stroke of his fingers, my attachment to him grew. Toby was the kind of boy I needed.

The woman reached for a handheld device and ran it over my shoulders and neck. I wasn't sure what it was, but it didn't bother me. "Since you mentioned you just found him, I'm scanning him for a microchip." She shook her head and said, "Nothing, so no way to trace his owner, if he has one. We already checked the missing pet sites and files and he's not listed anywhere."

There was nobody looking for me but I couldn't tell them that. It had been a long time since I had belonged to someone, but I wanted to belong to Toby. I felt such a strong connection to him and knew we were meant to be together.

Trish scribbled something on her clipboard and looked up at Toby and Karen. "Just keep an eye on him when you get home and if he gets worse, take him to the veterinary clinic."

I instantly tilted my head in Toby's direction.

Toby and Karen looked at each other and then she gazed at me. I was a dirty mess. I'd been hanging out in the fields and orchards along the road, waiting and hoping for someone. I'd gotten distracted chasing a rabbit and run into a sticky mudhole in the orchard a few days before. I rolled and rolled in the grassy pastures to get it off, but it had encased my fur like plaster. I hoped she'd overlook that and appreciate what was underneath all the dirt.

I imagined being part of their home, being Toby's friend, resting next to the fire I saw burning through the window when I first glimpsed him working outside.

I detected a flicker of joy in Karen's eyes before her lips curved into an enthusiastic smile.

And I felt my tail wag from side to side.

CHAPTER 9

Then

The next morning, it's clear Buddy has no intention of leaving my side. That's what I've called him, Buddy. I hope he lives up to the name. He follows me around all morning and when I point to the garage and tell him to stay, he tilts his head to the side like the action alone will answer his question. There is a softness to his brow, to the wispy hairs around his eyes, a calmness to his demeanor. He seems happy here.

Buddy's deep and soulful eyes make me think back to the puppy that was almost mine. He had the same eyes—expressive eyes full of understanding. There were eight puppies in that litter. I wish it had worked out so I would have had him with me all this time. I would have always had a friend, no matter where we moved. I wonder where they all ended up and if they are still with the owners who took them home or if they've had to move around to lots of different places like me.

He trails me outside, through the dewy green grass, and I again try to persuade him to stay in the yard, but he walks next to me as I head down the road. I guess he's walking to school with me, and I'm happy for the company.

Can I trust what my mom said? Will we stay in Riverside? As I look down at Buddy, I still don't know if I should be the one to take care of him. If I'm the right person for him to follow.

"We have to be super careful here," I say as we walk. "There's traffic on the road, so we need to stay well off of it." I move to the side of the road, my shoes crunching in the bits of asphalt-covered gravel. Buddy follows and I motion him to stay on my left side, closest to the field, so I'm between him and the road.

Buddy trots alongside me, expelling soft clouds of breath into the crisp morning air. The rhythm of his mild panting sets our pace. The way he holds his mouth open a bit with the tip of his pink tongue hanging out results in a wide smile between the dimples on each side of his jaw. His matted and dirty tail wags from side to side in a happy arc. It's quiet as we reach the still dormant orchard, except for the swish of his tail and the scamper of rodents in the brush. We pass by a field with a few cows munching on their breakfast. Buddy looks, but keeps walking.

We're almost at the end of the road when Buddy darts over a few feet and dips his mouth into the stream that runs alongside the edge of the fields. He laps up some water and hurries back to catch up with me, licking his face. He's surefooted and not limping at all today.

Instead of taking the vehicular bridge over the river, I guide Buddy to the worn walking trail that leads down to the edge of the river. "This is a safer way for us to get across the water," I say, pointing at the trail. Buddy glances at me and then sniffs the dirt and grass and meanders along the pathway. The cheerful babbling of the water over rounded rocks accompanies our soft footsteps until we get to the old wooden footbridge.

The call from Dad yesterday has been bugging me. I wish we could talk to each other without it being such an ordeal. Each time I start to miss him and wish he was around, we end up quarreling. When he asked how I was doing, I wanted to ask him what he thought about me playing baseball, but didn't get a chance before he went off on me.

I wish I understood him. How can he be so hard and angry one minute and in the next breath sound concerned for me? I never even said goodbye to him before we left. He can make me so mad, but at the same time, I feel bad for him, being on his own, without a family to come home to.

Mom seemed to be having such a good first day and then when I mentioned the call, her mood deflated. I hate that he can still do that to her, even from a distance.

And why is he still calling her all the time? They're keeping something from me and I wish they trusted me and could be honest. For all Mom's talk about a fresh start here, I'm not sure how I'm supposed to do that when they're both clearly hanging on to my past.

I glance over at Buddy and he turns his gaze to meet mine. He trusts me and I'm not sure I'm worthy.

We hike the trail up the bank, Buddy's tail wagging in a happy swish. Buddy beats me to the top and waits. I point to the left where the trail will connect up with the street that runs in front of the school. Buddy trots by my side, his nose working overtime. We reach the end of the trail and he studies the building and the students roaming around outside.

There are some tall trees across the street and I'm not sure what the rules are regarding dogs on the schoolgrounds.

"There's a dog following you," Evan declares, seriously, as if I'd not noticed Buddy's presence, heard his paws hit the sidewalk, or him shaking off itches as we've been walking along the pathway.

"I met him last night on my way home," I mutter, trying to appear unbothered. "It looks like he's been abandoned so we decided to give him a home," I say. Better to give the facts than anything else. I get the feeling Evan's looking for an annoying conversation.

"What would you want with a dirty old bedraggled dog?" Evan, with never a hair out of place, points at the mass of tangled fur on Buddy's backside. "He probably has fleas and other diseases. Looks like he came right from the Gulch." I have no idea what place he's referring to, but he's obviously not a fan of canine companions.

Jerry joins his friend and they both laugh. "What's his name, Dirty? Crusty? Chewbacca?" They cackle and laugh together.

The same frustration I felt when I was talking to my dad yesterday boils to the surface. I like Buddy, but it's more that I can't stand being ridiculed. My heart pounds as I take two purposeful steps forward. I want to wipe that silly grin off Evan's face and take the finger he's pointing at Buddy and bend it so far back it breaks. I start to move toward them and feel Buddy's snout tapping my leg. He whines and grabs my jeans with a gentle tug back toward the trees.

I take my eyes off Evan, who's confused by Buddy's reaction, walk off to the side and focus on Buddy. It's only then that I realize that my hands have begun to shake. I look over at Evan and Jerry and they're still sneering at us. When I disagree with someone, it sets off something inside me that's almost impossible to stop.

At my old school, I got into some trouble, but at the time I felt it was worth it. As the new kid at so many different schools, I learned if I showed strength and didn't take any guff, everyone would leave me alone. Word gets around a campus quickly, and if I swatted down the first attack, it thwarted any other issues. That's been my habit for so long, it seems natural to me. I feel Buddy's soft head beneath my hand and stroke it a few times and take a deep breath. How did he just manage to placate my anger?

Buddy touches his paw to my leg and licks my fingertips. The first bell rings and I know I have to get to class. I look at Buddy, not certain what he's going to do. He can't come to class with me.

I back away and watch as he sits on the grass next to the tree, his eyes staring into mine. I hurry across the street and turn back to look before going inside, but Buddy is still in the same spot.

*

Throughout my morning classes, I worry about Buddy.

My mind wanders to him at every chance it gets. I peer out of every window, but none of them are in view of the tree. I don't want him wandering off, getting lost, or picked up by animal control. I wonder if they even have animal control in Riverside. My mind is so preoccupied with him, I don't give much thought to baseball or Evan until the bell rings for lunch. Evan and Jerry sneer at me, glaring and whispering as I walk by them. Lyle invites me to join him, but I can't. I know I won't be able to focus until I see that Buddy's okay.

"I've got to run, but I'll see you at the tryouts tonight." I make sure I say it loud enough for Evan to hear me and watch as he shakes his head and flashes me a resentful glare. I grab another sandwich and snacks and head across the street.

As I approach, Buddy's still there. He raises his head and stares at me, his tail thumping on the ground. He hasn't budged from his spot and I run to him and sit with my back against the tree. Buddy greets me with enthusiastic licks as I tear off bits of meat and cheese and share my lunch with him.

With the sandwich and apple gone, I take one more drink of my water and pour the rest into Buddy's mouth. He places his head across my lap and I rub his ear between my fingers.

I've known Buddy for only a day, but I feel like I've known him for a lifetime. I don't think I've ever waited for anything for this long in my life, so what makes him think I'll keep coming back? Let him walk by my side? Bring him food? How can dogs rely on someone so quickly?

I glance across the street and find Evan at his spot at the fence. His eyes meet mine and convey nothing but contempt. Evan and Jerry are the type of kids who have to make fun of others so they feel better about themselves. The way they treated Buddy is a prime example.

It's not that I don't want anything to do with him, but maybe I don't need his kind of friendship. The therapist said I need to surround myself with positive people and make better choices when it comes to my actions and my friends but I hadn't really thought about it before now. My mom has said it time and time again. Dr. Hawes talked at length about impulse control and my lack of it. She said that the frontal lobe in my brain wouldn't fully form until I'm in my twenties and that is the part of the brain tasked with self-control and reason. Basically, she was saying I'm a child, but she hasn't lived with my dad, seen the things I've seen. I'm more of a man than she knows. She gave me some tools, wanting me to use more effective ways to express myself, like having a conversation with myself to determine why I'm really angry and then, if warranted, talk to the person and explain why I'm upset, instead of flying off the handle. She recommended physical exercise and relaxation techniques, like focused breathing, to deal with my anger.

During my sessions, I learned sometimes I react to something that has nothing to do with the root of my anger. Many times, it stems from interactions with my dad and I feel powerless to confront him, so I take it out on the first thing that upsets me. It's a constant battle for me. The therapist also said that stress triggers these responses and to say life has been stressful lately would be an understatement.

I look down at the top of Buddy's head and soak in the calmness he exudes, running my hand over his back. Focusing on him helps me forget about Evan and Jerry.

Lyle and the other guys on the team are likeable and friendly so maybe I just need to open up and find something I enjoy. Maybe it could be baseball. Buddy slaps his tail against my backpack in support of my decision.

I scratch him behind the ears for a few minutes, until I have to go back to school. I'll be gone for a couple of hours, but somehow, I know Buddy will still be here. He locks on to my eyes and an understanding passes between us. He makes no move to leave and settles back into the grass. I get the sense he plans to wait for me.

The bell rings as I reach the door and I meet up with Lyle at my locker. "So, are you ready for tryouts tonight?"

I wait for a few seconds. Lyle is a nice kid—the type of kid Mom hoped I'd meet around here—the kind of guy that could be a good friend to me. "I'll be there."

"I'll introduce you to all the guys," says Lyle.

I bob my head. "Yeah, that'll be great. I'll see you there."

*

I remember Dad watching a baseball game on television with a couple of his friends from work several years ago. They whooped and hollered, rooting for the Mariners and acting like they knew the players personally. The game went on for hours and I can still hear the admiration in my dad's voice when he'd cheer on a runner or marvel at a pitch. If I make the team, maybe he'll come watch me play.

The final bell rings and I rush out of class, in a hurry to get to tryouts.

"Hey, Emerald City." I run smack into Evan as I make the last corner for my locker. I take a few steps away and ignore him. I dash across the street to pick up Buddy, who is gnawing on a stick, watching people walk by, without a care in the world. He glimpses me and drops the stick, hurrying to my side. We jog across the schoolgrounds to the field, where the current team and prospective members are gathered. I tell Buddy to stay by the edge of the dugout. Lyle and another boy walk up to me as I'm giving Buddy his instructions.

Lyle bends down to pet Buddy. "Hey, boy." He turns to me. "I wouldn't have pegged you as a dog person." He continues to stroke Buddy's fur, but his curious eyes remain on me, his brow furrowed as he studies me.

"I didn't either, until yesterday. I found him on the way home from school. His name is Buddy."

He gives Buddy's ears a scratch. "I've always wanted a golden retriever. Our neighbor had one years ago and I used to play with him."

Lyle gestures to the boy next to him. "This is Chet. He's our catcher."

Chet, a stocky guy with freckles across his nose and cheeks, gets down on the ground and ruffles Buddy's fur. He looks up at me and says, "Hey, Toby. Glad you decided to try out." Both of them continue to pet the dog and talk to him. Buddy stretches out and rolls onto his back, placing his head in Chet's lap. Buddy swishes his tail back and forth as Lyle rubs the sides of his face and under his chin. Chet continues with an aggressive belly rub and a bit of roughhousing.

"Be careful, we had to get his leg checked yesterday, he was limping," I say.

"Sorry," Chet says, easing his hand away and rubbing Buddy's head. "I get carried away with dogs. I've always grown up having at least one dog around our orchard."

Neither of them comments on the mud that's still plastered to his fur. Buddy's long tongue takes a swipe at Chet's hand, urging him to continue. Chet laughs and says, "You're a good boy, Buddy." He turns to me and points at the locker room. "You'd better go get changed."

After donning some borrowed Goats' practice sweats and picking up a glove Coach Hobson loans me, I return to the dugout. I arrive just as Coach is whistling for everyone to gather around home plate. Chet and Lyle motion me to a spot they've saved between the two of them.

Coach Hobson tells us to warm up by running around the track, we do some stretches, and he puts us in groups stationed behind each of the bases to run quick sprints. He brings out some medicine balls and has us toss them to each other. The weight feels tough against my muscles—it's been a while since I've really done any sport and I'm not even sure I'm made for it, but I'm prepared to try.

Despite the chill in the air, I'm dripping with sweat and dry my hands on my sweats to keep the ball from slipping. We trade partners as we throw the medicine balls and the guys are friendly. I can tell most of them are already on the team, their movements through the drills fluid and practiced, their teasing banter with each other, and their unconcerned approach to the exercises. Those of us trying out are more reserved, taking our cues from the others, matching our motions and concentrating on doing things correctly, not saying much, beyond a quick greeting. As we move through the group, Coach Hobson reminds everyone there is a maximum of twenty players on the team and there are only three openings.

I do a quick count and realize there are six of us trying out. I've got a fifty-fifty chance.

After dividing into groups, Coach Hobson rotates us through running the bases, hitting balls, and catching. When I'm hitting, one of the guys comes over and shows me how I'm gripping the bat too tightly and demonstrates how to loosen my grip. As we go through the different drills, Coach calls each of us trying out over to him, one by one. I'm the last one he summons. He assumes the position of catcher and asks me to throw him the ball, while the other players continue the drills.

I throw my first ball and it smacks into his glove. "Good arm, Toby. You've never pitched before yesterday, right?"

"Right, sir."

"Again," he says, tossing me the ball.

I pitch him the ball again and again. He gives me pointers on my stance and release after each throw and the process feels good. I listen and apply his suggestions. He hollers for Chet to come over and serve as the catcher and Coach Hobson comes to stand with me.

He guides my arm and pitches the ball himself a few times to show me the techniques. After dozens of pitches, he seems impressed. He whistles to round up the team and they gather the equipment and make their way toward the dugout. He tells me to continue to throw balls to Chet.

With the rest of the team watching, which makes my pulse quicken and my stomach dance, I pitch a few more times, doing my best to ignore them and focus on how Coach told me to throw. The wallop reverberates across the field as the last ball I release lands in Chet's glove, and I take a seat with the others.

I join Lyle, who plays first base, and most of the other players sitting on the portable bleachers along the first base line. They clap when I arrive and pat me on the back as I take a seat. "Wow, you've got a great arm, Toby," Lyle says.

Coach points at two of the other kids who are trying out and motions them onto the field. He guides them through a similar process as he observes the boy who's covering third base. Coach Hobson employs the same methods and gives him tips on improving his throw to home plate. All the boys sitting on the bench watch and cheer the others on. Nobody makes fun of the boy when he drops the ball, or the third guy Coach is helping who takes a wild swing and misses. Coach watches over them and gives suggestions, moving arms, positioning shoulders.

In between chats with the other guys, turns out there's another boy from Seattle on the team, Andy, who moved here last year and lives with his grandparents. He assures me I'll adjust to living in Riverside and will only miss the variety of eateries. I glance over at the dugout and watch Buddy, sitting in the same spot, studying the activities. His eyes follow the ball so carefully as it flies from the pitching mound to home plate. Buddy's attention is never distracted by the loud noises we make, Coach's rough instructions. While we're all focusing on the hit, he follows the ball until it finds the ground.

From what I've seen of dogs, they're always running and chasing balls. I'm shocked Buddy hasn't dashed onto the field and tried to capture one. He seems enthralled with the game, almost like he's studying. I'm thankful he's not making a nuisance of himself, but I've never met a dog content to sit for so long while being tempted by balls flying and people running. He's no ordinary dog.

Coach finishes with the last boy—Jared, who Lyle tells me moved to Riverside this year from Oregon—and walks across the field to where we're sitting, grabbing Jared by the shoulder like he's his own son. "Great job, guys," he says as he comes to stand beside us, Jared taking an empty spot just in front of my feet. "I can tell some of you have been doing more than just sitting on the couch stuffing yourselves with holiday cookies this winter." He laughs and puts his foot on the first row of bleachers and leans in closer to us. "I fell in love with baseball when I was younger than all of you. I know, hard to believe… It's a magnificent game. One of finesse and patience. Being bigger and stronger isn't what always works in the game." He taps his forehead. "You've got to use your brain. It's your most powerful muscle."

He turns and looks across the field for a moment. "That field out there is my favorite place to be. It's the place I learned to never give up. To take things one step at a time and enjoy the moment." Lyle starts to laugh and points across the field. Buddy is past the outfield, tossing a stick into the air and catching it, then rolling around with delight. Coach follows Lyle's finger and chuckles along with the rest of us. "That guy knows how to enjoy himself…

Relish your games like that." He laughs. "The ones where you hit a home run or catch a ball and make a double play. Learn from each other. When you swing and miss, when you throw to the wrong base, figure out what you did and improve, so you don't do it again. Ask each other questions." He waves his hand across the bleachers and for the first time I regard the whole group together. "This is our team. We can all count on each other. We'll work together to do what's best for the team. You might be asked to give up something for yourself for the benefit of the team and I expect you to do so without a poor attitude."

He reviews our obligations for being part of the team, reiterating the academic requirements. "We'll have more fun than you can imagine, but I also have high standards. I'm not going to tolerate any misbehavior. If you can't conduct yourselves like gentlemen, I won't hesitate to boot you off the team, no matter how good of a player you are. Everybody understand?"

I nod and say yes, as do all the others sitting around me. Listening to him talk about baseball and what it means to him, I can't visualize not agreeing to whatever terms he suggests. He's unlike any coach I've ever encountered and his passion for the game is clear. I close my eyes and hope I get to be part of this.

I listen as he calls out Jared and another boy, Roberto, and congratulates them on making the team. Coach Hobson whistles to get our attention and stop the applause. My heart is pounding and my hands are sweating, as the confidence I was finding while Coach was praising me evaporates and turns to despair. There's only one more spot to fill. When I agreed to try out, I didn't expect to care about this so much. Playing baseball was never something I dreamed of doing. But there's an energy within the team and I liked how they helped and encouraged me. I already feel like I belong, not like an outsider.

When it's quiet, Coach continues. "As you all know, Steve moved away before Christmas, so we need a new pitcher. I think you'll all agree, Toby is our man. He's got a natural talent." He turns to face me. "We'd love to have you join the team."

It takes me a minute to understand what he's saying. "You mean, I made the team?"

Coach Hobson laughs and smiles. "That's right. Welcome to the Goats."

I can't believe it. Talk about not being invisible. I'll be the guy everyone is watching. I wipe my sweaty palms on my pants as a flicker of anxiety pulsates in my chest while the other guys pat me on the back. The pitcher? He's always in the spotlight. That's where the cameras focus on games I've watched on TV. That's the player who gets not only the accolades, but all the wrath from the fans. I remember Dad and his friends yelling at the screen when the pitcher made an error. If I make a mistake, everyone will see it.

I watch as Coach Hobson congratulates the players, gives them high-fives, or shakes their hands as they gather equipment and tote it back to the storage room. He makes a point of talking to each of the three kids who didn't make the team and when they walk away, they look encouraged, not rejected. I realize I'm staring slightly intently at him when he turns and walks over to me.

"Coach, look, I really appreciate this, and I don't want to let you down—"

"I've been coaching for over twenty-five years, Toby," he interrupts me, "and I can honestly say I've only had three kids show this much potential. Most of these kids have played since they were little tykes. It's rare to find a sophomore with your skills who has never been on a team." I appreciate what he's saying but there's no guarantee I can do anything with that. He continues. "Imagine what you'll be doing when you get some practice under your belt. Not to mention, my awesome coaching." He laughs and grips my shoulder.

Looking at him, it's too hard to refuse.

"I'll do my best," I say. "I just don't want to let you or the team down."

"Won't happen. I'll make sure you're ready." He reassures me by tightening his grip on my shoulder. "Just have your parents read the paperwork over—you need their approval to sign up. Bring the signed forms back to me tomorrow." Everything Coach says is with passion and emotion—as if games are his whole life—it's quite infectious, and I feel a sense of that rubbing off on me already.

I nod my understanding and stare over at Buddy. "Thanks, Coach."

A knot forms in my stomach. The cost of a glove. Something we definitely don't have.

"Uh, I'm not sure I can get a glove right away. Having never played before, I don't have any equipment."

"Not to worry," he says, "I've got a couple in my office. You can give them a try and choose whichever one works best. You shouldn't buy one until you know what you like." He flicks his head in Buddy's direction, where my faithful new friend is sitting up, his golden fur shimmering in the light from the setting sun. "Is that your dog?"

"Yes, sir. His name's Buddy. I'd tell him to get off the field," I say with trepidation—*what if he wants me to send him home?*— "but he seems to go where he wants and he's pretty intent on following me everywhere."

"I had a Labrador retriever once," he says almost absentmindedly. "They're the best dogs. Just make sure you clean up after him. I need to keep this field in perfect shape."

My backpack is heavy with homework, but I don't even notice it. Mom is going to be shocked. Instead of the dread and uncertainty I had faced about coming to a new school, I hold my head a little higher as I take each step with Buddy by my side and the two of us make our way to the river path.

CHAPTER 10

Now

Karen tells me it has been two weeks, fourteen days, since Toby's memorial service. I'm waiting in this quiet place, staring at the stone with Toby's name. The rich scent of moist soil wafts through the air and I lift my head and sniff. They had a service yesterday a few sections over and I watched them lower a casket draped with sweet-smelling blossoms into the ground. The earthy scent mixed with the perfume of all the flowers beckoned me near the grave last night. I stayed on the grass, so as not to leave any paw prints in the fresh dirt and cause a concern. I wouldn't want them to think someone, or something, had been trespassing. The not so distant howl of coyotes woke me last night and with winter coming, they're more active.

Karen left me a few minutes ago. She's losing patience with me. She comes every morning on her way to school and every afternoon on her way home. She makes sure I have food and water, brushes my coat, and sometimes sits with me. She tries her best to coax me to the car. The past few days she's been leaving a trail of treats and food, begging me to come with her.

Tears form in her eyes and I sense her worry and irritation, but I'm waiting for Toby, like I always have. I get up a few times a day, take care of business, stretch my legs, gobble up the bits of food Karen uses to lure me to her. I have to make sure I get to the food before those pesky squirrels. They taunt me enough without the attraction of kibble next to me. Years ago, I would have chased them with abandon, but I've got bigger things on my mind now.

The instinct to give chase when I spot one comes from deep in my brain. The prey drive to chase fast-moving objects like those irritating squirrels is strong, so strong that I have to fight to keep myself from jumping up and bounding after them. If I didn't have a bad hip and wasn't focusing all my attention on Toby, the squirrels wouldn't know what hit them. Not that I'd catch them, but chasing them is thrilling. In my younger days, squirrels had more respect for me. Every so often, when I'm feeling spunky, I wait for them to draw near me and steel myself to jump up and leap toward them. I like to let them know I'm unpredictable, which is like Toby's job as a pitcher. He is supposed to surprise the hitter with his pitch. That's what I'm doing with the squirrels.

I always wanted my own squirrel, but they're hard to catch.

Loads of people come to meet you when you're a young pup, nestling near your mother, waiting for your new home, but they never looked at me the way Toby did. The connection I have with him is one I've never experienced. His eyes softened whenever he looked at me, his voice mellowed when he talked.

You can tell so much about a person by looking into their eyes. In Toby's eyes I saw a boy—he may have pretended he could handle the world, but he was still growing up, still learning who he could trust in this world, and still figuring out that some people need a little more patience and kindness.

It had been so long since I'd felt the warmth of love from a person. Like the prey drive, the pack drive is an overwhelming instinct hardwired in the cells of my body. I longed to be part of a pack. I needed to be with someone like Toby and work with him, help him. Goldens, in particular, have a high pack drive. That's why I follow Toby everywhere. I'm his constant companion. He's my family.

I'd always wanted a family—I'd been on my own for a long time you see—just surviving as best I could. To have somewhere safe and warm, with loving people, meant more to me than Toby will ever know. I know he was scared that he wouldn't be with me for long, but in life we can't care about that, can we? Sometimes you get mere moments with a person, sometimes we get a lifetime, but someone can change your life in the briefest fragment of time, and having that is better than nothing. It's better than being alone forever.

During those early days in the house with Toby and Karen, I learned more about their household. Toby carried a great deal of anger inside him and I sensed that the moment I met him. Anger, sadness, guilt, and regret emanated from him. It was a heavy burden and I think he'd been carrying it for far too long. Sometimes just hearing his mom mention his dad caused his breathing to increase and his heart to pound. I cued into this and tried to distract him with a nudge from my nose or a pull on his shirt. It was like his brain couldn't think clearly. It was locked in the limbic mode, leaving him with only two solutions—fight or flight. The anger overriding all rational thought.

I could tell by Karen's conversations with Toby, she was concerned about him.

But even in your darkest moments, there is hope that can be found.

I always felt Toby longed for someone to spend time with.

It's important for a man, young or old, to have a woman in his life. I can always tell the difference between a house where a man lives alone and one where a man is in a relationship with a woman. Instead of being just a structure, it feels warmer, softer, more welcoming.

I had an owner once who didn't look after himself, and I lost him.

Life can be lonely and, in the beginning, I wasn't sure Toby even trusted Karen: for all the good she'd done for him, she'd been his only constant in life, and I think Toby believed everyone would leave at some time or another.

And what he felt was true. I know I'll have to let go of Toby myself one day.

If I could talk, I would have said something encouraging and reassuring to Toby in those first nights, but instead I licked his hands and moved closer to him at every chance I got, so he always knew I was there. I'll always be there for my boy.

I still sense that strong connection to Toby, even today. Everyone else has given up on him. I'm not leaving as long as I know he's still out there somewhere. Deep inside, I can feel him.

CHAPTER 11

Then

I always wanted a brother. Someone I could sit with on the front porch when Mom wasn't back from work. Someone to joke with and get annoyed with, who was going through everything I was. Someone to share a tent in the backyard and read scary stories with, to experiment in the kitchen and make chocolate-chip banana pancakes with, someone to help me explore every new place we moved to. But now I have Buddy.

I whistle for Buddy, grabbing my backpack and finding him waiting for me at the door. Spring is pretty beautiful in Riverside, even I can't deny that. The dormant orchards are done hibernating and the trees are decorated with delicate blossoms in pink and white hues. Mom's been planting like crazy in the backyard and I know more about gardening than I care to admit. But the gentle breeze always carries their perfume and I take a deep breath of the fresh scent every day.

The narrow stream that runs along the roadway is fed by the snow atop the mountains that surround the valley and it's now trickling with the first runoff of the season. My shoes and Buddy's paws are damp from the morning dew lingering on the grass alongside the road, and our morning walks are almost silent, permeated only by the sounds of chirping birds, the occasional chatter among the sheep and cows, and the plod of Buddy's feet.

When we moved here, I thought the silence would drive me mad, but I've come to enjoy the peaceful nature of this little town.

The drab colors of winter are gone, with the brilliant shades of green sprouting from the dark earth of the fields. The massive bigleaf maple on the corner is starting to flower with greenish-yellow clusters hanging from the branches. The entire valley surrounding Maple Lake is blooming. It's full of hope and promise, and baseball, of course.

Buddy holds his head high and takes in our surroundings, as always, keeping close by my side. As the seasons change, his nose goes into overdrive, sniffing the newest additions on our route. I don't mind, if I'm not running late, but if I'm in a hurry, all I have to do is tell him to get moving and he leaves whatever new weed or enticing bit of fresh manure has captured his attention and hurries back to my side.

My morning walks to school with Buddy have become the best part of my day. His gentle eyes remind me I'll never be alone. He's a faithful companion who never tires of being near me. He's an excellent listener and sometimes, the way he looks at me, I think he understands me even when I don't say a word.

When I get to school, I bend down and give Buddy a good scratching. His coat is thick and shiny, his feathers on his belly and tail long and untangled. His thick fur gleams in the morning sunlight and while his chest is blonder now, his back and face are darker with hints of copper. As the golden strands glimmer in the morning light, it's easy to understand how his breed got its name. As he takes long, smooth strides, his magnificent banner of a tail flicks from side to side. Now that he's eating regularly, he's put on some weight and his ribs are no longer visible. Only when I run my hands along his back and push through his thick coat can I detect them. He gets a bath every week or two and I trim his nails once a month. He lets me massage his paw pads with a cream that keeps them soft and supple. Chet's always complaining about having to wash his border collie, Bandit, but Buddy relishes it: his eyes close and his mouth hangs open when I massage his neck and head.

Unlike last year when he first came to live with us and waited for me at school, we've transitioned to a new routine. After wandering with me each morning, Buddy spends the day at home, using the doggy door we installed for him when his toenails had scratched Mom's doorframe one too many times. Buddy meets me each day after school, either at the baseball field during our practice season or at the spot I first found him, on the road to our house—I always spot him there, come rain or shine, with new mud embedded in the space between his toes or bits of grass and weeds from some adventure sticking along his back legs.

I've been able to juggle my schoolwork with practice. It's easier during the off-season, but I've got a good handle on my classes and for the first time in my life I feel successful. We've had a great season this year and are undefeated, so far.

Engineering is my favorite class, which I can't even believe. It started with mechanical drafting where we had to do all our drawings by hand, using compasses and scales. The intricacies of the work help me focus, and are gratifying. Mr. Mills believes in learning the principles and is a stickler for making sure we understand the basics before he introduces the modern computer software. Doing everything by hand is tedious, but when I finish a drawing, I feel a real sense of accomplishment.

The computer software we use is fast and easy—we've been designing basic machines, bridges, and structures and it's the first time I've found something I'm really good at in school. The designs and calculations are second nature to me, almost effortless. I remember all the times I've had to fix things around the house or put together things with all those little packets of screws and nuts and pages of instructions. I never bother reading the directions, I can just look at all the parts and pieces and assemble it. Mom's always amazed because, while she's still reading, I'm usually done with the whole project. Without realizing it, I've been practicing these same skills we're using in class.

I'm not entirely on board with having to take physics this year, though apparently it will help me excel in engineering. I'll be lucky if I get through it with a passing grade.

The bell rings for lunch and I meet up with Lyle and Chet, like I always do. I haven't told them about Dad but he's further from my thoughts these days and his instructions don't repeat in my mind so often. The orchard Chet's parents own is even more calming and I got my first taste of farm life at Lyle's. Both of them have tons of chores to do to help run their family businesses, but they always include Buddy in the invitation to their homes and I can tell he loves to visit.

Buddy can run through the orchard and play with the apples that have fallen on the ground. Lyle's family has chickens, horses, a few cows, sheep, and a couple goats. On our first visit, Buddy was inquisitive and intimidated by the larger animals, grumbling when he spotted them, raising the hairs on his back when they made noises, but now he's comfortable. He's got a favorite friend in a horse named Wink. The shiny black horse always rushes to the fence to greet Buddy when we arrive. Lyle's dad has a black Labrador retriever called Smudge who's out in the fields.

Lyle and Chet have come to our house a couple of times, but I go to theirs more often. With all their chores, it's difficult for them to get away, and when I'm there, I help them so the work goes faster. I never thought I'd enjoy the outdoors so much, but I've felt a sense of peace here I never had in the city… with the wind whipping and my shoulders straining from the chores it's like the anger built up inside me from years with my dad just melts away.

I can't get the conversation I had with my math teacher this morning out of my mind. "Ms. Wright thinks I'll probably end up with a baseball scholarship to college." I pick up my tray and follow them to a table.

"There's no way I could go to college without a scholarship. We couldn't afford it, so I hope she's right." I take my first bite of the warm dough of my pizza, covered with red sauce and pepperoni. I have contemplated the idea of Dad contributing to my college costs and always come to the same conclusion: It's not going to happen. Mom is still struggling, and I'm too scared to talk to him. He phones Mom a few times a month but I make myself scarce and take Buddy for a walk, or refuse the invitation Mom extends with her eyes.

She usually tries to prod me to talk to him, but I'm not interested. I've ignored all of his calls when his name pops up on my cell phone and tell myself I'll call him later. I feel guilty dodging him, but I never know what to say. The last thing I want to do is argue with him. I'm sure he's lonely and there are times I think he calls because he misses us. When I think about him alone in his bunk or sitting in an empty house, I get a lump in my throat. It's not that I don't love him. He's my dad and I'll always love him, but we can't seem to have a normal conversation and I always say something that sets him off. When Mom talks to him, worry fills her face and the tension in her voice is unmistakable. I know something's not right and I keep hoping everything will be okay.

"Ms. Wright's got a point. You're the best pitcher we've had. I think there's no doubt you'll get a scholarship," Lyle replies and I'm distracted from my thoughts. "Coach Hobson will make sure of it. He always helps his players who want to go to college and has a great relationship with all the scouts," he says. "My cousin got a scholarship a few years ago to Ohio, with Coach's help."

Gratitude envelops me. Lyle's always the first player to leap to his feet and cheer a teammate on. When it's time to gather the equipment, he's the guy who will stay late and make sure it's all put away in the cabinets. He's an amazing athlete and can keep his toe on the base and stretch to catch the worst of throws. He's saved me a time or two by getting a player out when I've allowed a hit I shouldn't have. He does all this without taking credit or making us feel like we made a mistake. He always has a word of encouragement for any of us who are struggling, and I'm trying to be more like him, but I've spent so long on my own it's hard to open up to people, to let them in. Either I'm more like my dad than I realize or he's had more of an effect on me than I care to admit.

Unlike Chet and Lyle, who have felt like friends from the first day of practice, a couple of the guys on the team were a little less willing to accept me. One of them, Ollie, wanted to be the main pitcher, so he had some hard feelings. He and his best friend, Warren, made their issues known. They never said a peep when we were on the field or within earshot of Coach, but they liked to whisper with their friends in the halls.

It was hard, but I ignored them, remembering that Coach wanted us to put the team first. I didn't want to jeopardize my position on the team and I wasn't going to be a tattletale and run to Coach with it. It went on for a couple of weeks, until one day before practice, I saw Lyle talking to Ollie behind the dugout and after that Ollie's attitude disappeared. Coach had Ollie and I work together often on pitching drills and while I wouldn't say he's one of my best friends, we get along now. Enough. While Ollie and Warren never apologized, they did both come to the mound after our first win and congratulated me on my pitching. They took some time to warm up to me, but we've gotten along ever since.

"Yeah, and my oldest brother went to Arizona and Coach Hobson helped him," added Chet. "You'll have to start looking at schools you like with a baseball team," he continues.

"I need to find one with an engineering program. I think I'd like to do that. Mr. Mills has told me a few of the schools he recommends for it, so I'll have to research them too. I haven't given it much thought till now—I didn't expect to be able to go."

"You should go talk to Mrs. Norman in the library. She's in the office next to the librarian. She has a bunch of scholarship and career information," suggested Chet.

*

I get a pass from my last period teacher for the library to check out scholarships like Chet suggested. I make my way to the library, housed in the opposite end of the building from the gymnasium. I've been in here a handful of times and scan the area beyond the circulation desk. Behind a desk sits a stout woman with overpermed, bronze-tinted hair, laughing with a deep, throaty chuckle at something on her computer screen. Books cover every surface, spilling from the bookcases along the walls and stacked on tables and the corners of her desk.

She catches sight of me and motions me inside. The wall behind her is plastered with a collage of photos of people in graduation caps and gowns. She follows my gaze and says, "Those are all my kids." She chuckles and adds, "Not really, but I think of them as mine. They're all the kids I've helped get scholarships. That's my only requirement for helping them—a college graduation photo." She stands and moves toward the wall and I realize she's got to be six feet tall, with a personality that exceeds her height. She points at a few of the photos and tells me the names of the students and where they went to college.

"So, sit down and let's talk about you, Toby." She gestures to the chair in front of her desk.

"You know my name?"

She winks and says, "There's not much that goes on around here that I don't know. I would have had to have been living under a rock not to know our star pitcher." She asks me a few questions, noting my interests and my mother's place of employment on the form she's filling out, before she pulls up my grades on her computer. While she scrutinizes her screen, I notice all the Far Side cartoons taped to her file cabinets.

"It looks like you do well in math and science, but could bump up the English and Spanish grades a bit. My guess is you're squeaking by with a B- because of Coach Hobson." She gives me an inquisitive look over the bright red glasses she's wearing, attached to a beaded rhinestone chain around her neck.

"Yes, ma'am, I struggle the most with those subjects. Anything to do with reading and writing. They're not as interesting to me, I guess."

"With your mother being a teacher, I'm sure you've got a house full of books. Maybe you just haven't found the right story to spark your interest yet." She taps the keys on her keyboard. "Most of my favorite adventures are between the pages of a book."

Must be a thing with people who work in schools.

She scribbles a few notes on the form and turns her attention back to me. "I'll run your parameters through the computer and see what we can come up with for schools that have good engineering programs, a baseball team, and offer athletic scholarships. I'll talk to Coach Hobson and find out if he has any specific recommendations based on your baseball talents." She stands, pats my shoulder, and promises to get in touch with me soon. On my way out the door, she hands me two books. "Take a look at these and give them a try. They might change your mind about books." I look at the spines lettered with *To Kill a Mockingbird* and *The Martian*. It's safe to say I haven't read either one.

"You can take as long as you want, don't worry about the due date. Let me know what you think and if you don't like them, I'll find some others." She sends me on my way with a grin.

I'm not sold on the idea of reading if it's not required for class, but smile and take the books. Something tells me Mrs. Norman wouldn't take no for an answer.

*

Buddy is waiting for me at his spot by the dugout. Buddy's not like most dogs. He never ventures off to explore or gets distracted by anything blowing by in the grass. He's focused. He watches the game and watches me. He's always in the same spot, waiting, never whining or causing trouble. He's been to every practice and every home game.

All the guys on the team have come to think of Buddy as our unofficial mascot and have gotten used to him sitting by the dugout watching our practices, but even I was surprised when we took our positions for our first home game and Nate in left field spotted Buddy among the trees. Sometimes I wonder what he thinks as he watches us practice and play. He's so earnest and focused when he's at the field, as if he's analyzing each play, remembering it for the future. I often wonder if he played catch before I met him. I think for Buddy to be in the shape he was in, he hadn't played much of anything for a long time.

We're playing the Tigers on Friday. They're a tough team and Coach Hobson works us hard as we prepare for it. Chet and I have to be in sync, as the pitcher and catcher. We communicate using our eyes and the subtle hand signals Chet displays as he crouches on the ground.

When I'm waiting to practice hitting, I spend time sitting with Buddy. I explain some of the strategies we use and predict the types of pitches that will be thrown. Buddy watches with intensity and keeps his eye on the ball as it flies through the air. I call out the fastball pitches Coach Hobson delivers. He follows them with a changeup. I point to it as the hitter swings and misses. "See, Buddy, that's what it's all about. Coach says hitting is about timing and the pitcher's job is to disrupt that timing. That changeup is slower and the hitter took a swing too soon."

Buddy watches where I point and looks at me with such concentration, I'm certain he understands what I've told him. I grab a baseball and show him the grips for the pitches as Coach Hobson delivers them. I demonstrate the split-finger I've been working on, showing Buddy how my fingers are positioned apart along the seams. "I use this one when I want to coax a swing and a miss. It looks like a fastball, but dives down at the last second."

Buddy studies the ball and stares into my eyes as I tell him how Chet and I work together. Chet enjoys giving a bunch of signals to try to confuse our opponents. I know when he touches the bill of his cap, the next signal is real. Coach Hobson was right when he said my brain is going to be the most important muscle I use as a pitcher. Buddy turns back to watch Coach throw another ball.

I love pitching the fastball, but Coach has taught me the subtle nuances of grips and releases that make all the difference when trying to throw off my opponent at the plate. He works with Chet and me before each game to go over the hitters on the opposing team. We size them up and plan for the types of pitches we know will expose their weaknesses, but it's all fluid, depending on the status of the game. I never knew there was so much finesse that went into it.

After practice, Buddy and I make our walk home. The days are getting longer and there's still light in the sky. Lyle's cousin gave us permission to use one of the fields along his property as long as we keep it secure. Buddy and I cross over the narrow creek separating the field from the roadway and I apply pressure on the heavy wire looped around the post and open the gate. Buddy rushes through. He prances into the field and runs several yards away, confident that I will be throwing him a pitch.

I practice several throws and Buddy retrieves each one of them, bounding through the new growth of alfalfa and grass to return the ball. As we play, his smile gets bigger, his tongue seems to grow longer as he pants a bit heavier. I toss my last pitch and

Buddy brings it back. I let him carry the ball until we leave the field. It's my signal our game is over. Once I've secured the gate, I take the ball and Buddy slurps up water from the fresh stream. By summer, the water will be flowing much harder, but now it's just more than a trickle.

Mom is in the kitchen working on dinner and talking on her phone when we get back.

"I can't keep having the same conversation over and over, William. We're doing well here and this is not productive. There is no point in involving Toby, he's focused on school and baseball and that's how it needs to stay." She turns from the pan on the stove, sees me, and drops the spoon she's using. "I've got to go now." She disconnects the call. "How was your day?"

I let the moment pass, but threads of what she said about not involving me creep into my thoughts. I've been pushing Dad away, and maybe so has she. It reminds me of the guest speakers we had in our gym class this week. They were talking about depression and substance abuse, how to see the signs and help someone in pain. Some of what they said made me think of Dad. He seems out of control sometimes and so sad at others. They talked about how depression can change a person into someone you no longer recognize. The woman who spoke lost her son to suicide because he was severely depressed. She told us she lives with the pain and guilt and wishes she had recognized what was happening sooner. She said her son made it difficult to communicate with him and his mood swings were hard to handle.

I wonder if Dad is dealing with something like that. I've seen him drink a beer or two, but never overdo it, so I don't think he's an alcoholic, but I'd be the last to know. Maybe I should call him and ask how he's doing. But I never know what to say and if he is depressed, I don't want to say the wrong thing and make it worse. Even more, I don't want to make him angry, since it seems that's what I do best.

Mom's chattering on about scholarships. "You're so talented with those designs—I've seen that project in your bedroom," she says, breaking up my thoughts. "I wonder if someday you'll be famous like Leonardo da Vinci or Thomas Edison. Maybe you'll invent something we can't live without." As she stirs the meat for tacos, her voice betrays her excitement. "You've always been so good with fixing things and figuring things out, it stands to reason you'd be drawn to engineering." She pauses and with increased enthusiasm says, "Oh, oh, maybe you can work with that Elon Musk guy on those electric cars. You'll still need good grades to get into school, even with a baseball scholarship, so be sure and stay up on your classes."

I load up my plate with several tortillas. "I know, Mom." I'm not sure I'll be in the same league as da Vinci or Edison, but I don't want to burst her bubble. It's good to be the reason she's happy.

As we finish dinner, she reminds me that she's going with Molly and Ginny from the café to a wine event at the library. She rambles on about the local wineries and restaurants that are taking part in the fundraiser and what she's going to wear.

I love the lilt in her voice and the gleam of happiness on her face. Should I ask her about the phone call with Dad? It's obvious she didn't want me to know and I hate to dampen her good spirits. I'll find a better time to broach the subject. She has more of a social life in this tiny town than she did the whole time we lived in Seattle. She's hit it off with the two sisters from the café and is in the habit of spending part of her weekends on outings with them. During the summer months, they usually come over at least once a week and sit around the table on the patio, visiting and laughing with Mom, while they cook up something delicious in our kitchen.

Back in Seattle, Mom was always on edge, never relaxed, even when Dad was gone. It's been too long to remember since Mom has enjoyed herself with friends. The only people that came to our old house were a couple of the neighbors, and except for the bond they shared being Navy wives, they never seemed that close to Mom. The constant tension we experienced in the city is gone but life is full of surprises.

CHAPTER 12

I've never been a fan of rallies and on Friday afternoon, during last period, there's a huge one in the gym right before our big game against the Tigers. I always avoided attending them back at my old school, but there's no sneaking away when you're part of the team and the whole reason for the excitement.

The pep squad and cheerleaders are in charge of the assembly and they escort the team onto the court and introduce us. The bleachers that line both sides of the gym are filled with students sporting green and gold shirts, waving banners, and cheering.

The entire student body engages in the games and skits, either participating or applauding. The captain of the pep squad calls students out of the audience and I'm lined up with a few of my teammates, across from some of the cheerleaders. They blindfold the players and give each of us one end of a super long fruit rollup. The cheerleader across from us is given the other end. We have to chew it as fast as we can until we meet in the middle where the first pair to finish the fruit will be declared the winners. The crowd whoops and hollers, leaping to their feet. I have no idea if I'm winning or losing, but when my nose connects with the face in front of me, I slip off my blindfold to discover not a cheerleader, but Lyle. I'm embarrassed at first, but then everyone laughs and we all take it in stride as a good joke.

Even the teachers get involved and do a funny dance to encourage us, which makes everyone roar with laughter. Coach Hobson kisses Peanut, one of the pygmy goats, to bring us luck and the crowd goes hysterical. The cheerleaders and dance club get everyone on their feet cheering for the Goats and the band escorts us to the field. Our teams are tied, both undefeated for the season and the pressure to win is intense.

The weight of that pressure sits firmly on my shoulders and my stomach has been doing somersaults all day. I guess that's the purpose of the rally: a distraction. You'd think Coach would be against it, but he joins in the fun—he's always telling us not to waste our energy worrying, but that's easier said than done.

As the gym empties and I watch the students make their way to the field, waving banners and pompoms, I know how important it is to the whole town that we win. I take a deep breath, determined to focus on my performance and what I can control. The grandstands are filling with spectators as I warm up in the bullpen. Coach Hobson meets with Chet and me one more time before the game begins. "Slow and steady, boys. Use your head and stay focused on what's in front of you," he says, clasping each of us on the shoulder. "Remember to take it one batter at a time."

It's a flawless April afternoon. The sun is shining and the sky is a perfect clear blue with a scattering of fluffy white clouds. I survey the grandstands. I've never seen this many spectators for one of our games. The Riverside bleachers are overflowing and the sea of orange shirts on the other side of the field makes me think most of the Tigers' fans are here.

Come the bottom of the ninth inning we're ahead by one run. I take the mound and try to shut out the yelling and actual growling coming from the Tigers' fans and the loud pounding of feet against the metal bleachers from our side of the field. In between all of this chaos, our band plays our school fight song and the clash of the cymbals rings in my ears. I need to stop the Tigers from getting a run. I know my teammates will do all they can to tag them out if they get a hit, but I'm focused on keeping them from advancing. I welcome the breeze that cools the back of my neck and aim my eyes at home plate.

Chet and I lock eyes and he communicates a signal for the batter in between us. I tilt my head in agreement and touch my foot to the rubber, pivot, and release a smoking fastball.

"Strike one," yells the umpire.

I toss the ball in my glove as I ready myself for the next pitch. This kid has a hard time with fastballs, so Chet specifies the same pitch. Another strike and our fans erupt in applause. One more, that's all I need. I move my cap and let the breeze cool my hairline. Chet taps the brim of his cap and indicates a new pitch. I give him a slight nod and position the ball in my hand.

I close my eyes, remembering all the times I've practiced this exact pitch. I block out the noise of the crowd and concentrate on the whisper of the air across my ears, take a few calming breaths, and envision the ball sailing through the air landing exactly where I intend. I know it has to be faster than a curveball and just a little slower than my fastball. I adjust my grip, as this one depends on the pressure I apply from my fingertips. I deliver a perfect slider that drops off at a downward angle as it reaches the plate. The batter swings and misses. Third strike.

The crowd continues to go wild and I home in on the next batter. I remember him from a previous game and Chet and I have studied him. He's one of their better hitters, but he's also cocky and tends to think he can hit any ball. That's a weakness I want to expose. We start with a splitter and he swings at it, but misses. I don't think he'll expect the same pitch again and neither does Chet, so that's what he gestures. The Tiger swings again. Another miss, but he was close.

Chet changes it up to a fastball, hoping the batter is ready for another splitter. He swings and the sound I dread—the smack of the bat connecting with the ball—echoes across the field. He didn't get much of a bite on it and the ball flies high into the air, and before it hits the ground Lyle steps from his position at first base and the ball plops into his glove. Lyle is all smiles as the spectators go crazy. Two outs. One more to go.

Another top hitter from the Tigers steps up to the plate. Chet and I discussed this guy and have a plan in place. My catcher nods to me to indicate to keep with our plan. I throw an intentional ball the first time, fast and inside. He thinks I'm tired and the stress is getting to me. He smirks with confidence. I don't delay and pitch the next one, a strike that breaks low and away. One ball, one strike.

I throw another inside ball that backs the batter up and irritates him. He's anxious to hit, so I throw him a changeup, which is just a little slower than my fastball and he swings too soon. Strike two. A trickle of sweat runs down the length of my back. My heart pounds in my throat and I take a few deep breaths and look over at the grove of trees. Buddy is sitting in his usual spot, eyes locked onto me.

I focus my attention on the batter. I don't want him to hit the ball, because he's known to hit home runs. I don't want a tie game and overtime. I want to strike this guy out. Chet and I agree on the pitch. I know the most important thing to do is use my hand speed to transfer leverage to the front of the ball. I concentrate and position my fingers for the pitch I use the least and the one I find most difficult to throw. I focus my thoughts and energy on my form and release the perfect curveball, which causes the batter to swing and miss. I hear the sweetest words ever uttered from the umpire. "Strike three. You're out."

The crowd comes to their feet, stomping even louder on the metal bleachers. The school song blasts from the band section and the cheerleaders lead everyone in chanting for the Goats. The players rush to the mound and slap me on the back, tap me with their gloves, and talk to me all at once, but I can barely hear a thing, the adrenaline from the game still coursing through me. We line up, like Coach taught us, and file over to the Tigers' dugout, shaking hands with each player.

When I get back to our dugout, Coach is waiting, smiling from ear to ear. He's got an arm around Chet. He reaches for me and engulfs me in a one-armed hug. "Incredible job, both of you," he says warmly. I know he's won before but his enthusiasm never wanes. "Way to keep them off balance. You guys were great."

Before I know it, each of us is grabbed by our teammates and hoisted on someone's shoulders. From high above the crowd, I spot Mom, along with Ginny and Molly, who are waving their banners and shouting my name.

My feet don't touch the ground until I'm in the locker room where we're all reliving our favorite moments of the game while we're getting changed. Coach Hobson is treating us to pizza to celebrate our victory.

After I change, I push open the heavy locker room door and scan the sidewalk for Buddy and I notice a girl I've never seen before. Her dark hair is long and shiny even from a distance. She's rubbing Buddy's chin and scratching his ears. His eyes are closed, his lips curved in a huge smile, and he's savoring the attention. The urge to introduce myself to her is strong, but I'm unable to muster the nerve. I can't think of anything to say and opt to call Buddy away. His head turns and she gives Buddy one more caress before hurrying away in the opposite direction.

Maybe she's a friend of one of the girls visiting for the weekend or something, but I don't have time to wonder for too long. Besides, I'd remember if I'd seen her before.

CHAPTER 13

Saturday morning, after Mom cooks a celebratory breakfast (pancakes piled high with golden syrup that sticks all over my face), Buddy brings me a ball and drops it at my feet. It's his not so subtle signal. I'm drained from yesterday, but can't resist Buddy's pleading eyes. I know he'd rather play in the field where he can run a long distance, but the backyard is where we play when we don't have time to make the walk down the road.

I pick up the ball and head outside, where the yard is bursting into bloom. Mom was right about the mixture of colorful flowers. I helped her tote them home from the nursery, and wedge in the metal stakes she'd made with the names of the flowers on them. She was definitely trying to encourage me to learn more about them. The brilliant blue and purples with a few yellow lilies interspersed certainly makes the patio look more impressive. The grass is beginning to green, and Buddy takes up his position at the far end of the yard, waiting for my throw. It's a gentle game today and after a few tosses and retrievals, I notice a slight limp, a little spasm on the muscle in Buddy's leg as he runs. It's the same leg he favored on the day I found him in the road, and as I sit on the grass and motion for Buddy to come, a feeling of worry starts to invade me.

Though I detect nothing, when he stands and walks, he continues to limp and he's not putting any weight on that paw. "Did you hurt yourself jumping into Coach's truck last night?" I ask and as if in response, Buddy licks the lower part of his leg and paw.

I poke my head inside and ask Mom to find a vet that can get Buddy in today. While we wait, I brush Buddy's fur. He sighs as he moves on his side so I can groom the feathers on his belly. As I'm finishing up, making sure his backside is tangle-free, Mom hollers out the door that the vet can take him first thing.

"Come on Buddy, let's go." The clinic is just a block off the main route we take to school, right before the bridge over the lake.

Buddy doesn't normally wear a leash, but the vet requires all dogs to be on one and I make sure and attach it to his collar before I take him inside. I check in with the receptionist behind the counter, and as I'm turning to find a seat, I see her.

The girl I saw after the game on Friday.

She comes around the corner from the back office and sits down in the chair next to the receptionist. She's not paying attention, her eyes focused on the paperwork on the desk. Her dark hair looks straighter, longer today, with wisps of it framing her face as she concentrates.

I sit down to wait and focus on the top of her head behind the high counter. The older woman speaks in an impatient voice. "This is where you enter the pet's name and the reason for the appointment." The keys on the keyboard clack. "We block out twenty minutes for most appointments and the types of appointments are color-coded in this table."

The phone rings and the girl answers, "Riverside Veterinary Clinic." Her voice is soft and sweet with a lilt at the end of her greeting.

After a few minutes, a technician comes through and studies the chart she's holding. "Buddy," she says, looking at us.

She glances at the reception counter and says, "Natasha, come with me and you can help with this patient." Natasha. She leads us to an examination room and Natasha follows, absentmindedly. I don't think she's spotted me yet.

The technician introduces herself as Rachel and motions us into an exam room. Natasha follows and bends down to look Buddy in the eye.

"I remember you, big guy. What's the matter?" She ruffles his neck with her hands and he hangs out his tongue. She turns her gaze to me and winks. "Buddy and I go way back, we met last night."

Her eyes are so blue. "After the game, right?" I ask.

She nods, still petting Buddy, who is enamored with her. As Rachel asks a few questions and jots down notes in Buddy's chart, I explain when the limp started. Rachel shows Natasha what she's written in the chart and explains it.

"Okay, the doctor will be right in." Rachel glances at Buddy, who is leaning against Natasha, letting her massage his ears. Her eyes flit to Natasha's. "You can wait here with Buddy and help the doctor."

When the door closes, Natasha continues to stroke Buddy, but focuses on me. "You're the pitcher for the baseball team, aren't you?"

"Right," I say, in a voice a few octaves higher than normal. I clear my throat and add, "I'm Toby. Toby Fuller." I rub Buddy's back.

She smiles and I smile back too. "He's so cute," she says. "I saw you call to him after the game."

"Right," I reply, pausing for a moment to think of what to say next. "He goes with me everywhere. Since the day I found him on the road walking home from school." I watch her as she scratches under Buddy's chin. "I haven't seen you at school. Are you new to town?"

She laughs, "Yes and no. I come every summer, but will be starting school here on Monday. My dad's the vet." She gestures with her head toward the door. "My mom decided it would best for me to live with him for a bit." She rolls her eyes. "I voted for staying home alone while my mom travels, but that got vetoed."

I shake my head and say, "Parents, right?" That explains the mystery. "I just moved here last year. Seattle."

"Ah, so you're used to a bigger town, too? I'm hoping I can adjust to this place full-time. I always have fun in the summers, but living here could be a different story. There's not much to do." She offers Buddy a dog cookie, and he accepts without reservation. "Denver was a lot more fun, particularly for a junior."

My mind is racing to think of something else to say as I take in her openness. I wish I had that sense of calm. Mind you, sometimes we pretend to be calmer than we really are. Maybe she just knows what to say. You can't always tell how someone feels on the inside from what they portray.

Her casual way of describing her home life gives me hope that maybe mine won't always feel so awkward. The door opens and the doctor's arrival interrupts my thoughts.

Dr. Thompson introduces himself and explains that Natasha will be working at the clinic on weekends and after school. He reviews Buddy's chart and starts the examination by taking his temperature, explaining to Natasha how she should hold Buddy. She follows his instructions, sits on the floor, and puts her hands around Buddy's shoulders, saying sweet things as she moves closer to him. "Remember, Natasha, not too tight, you'll make him nervous." She loosens her hold on him and smooths his ears.

Buddy tolerates the thermometer, and I pet his head and reassure him as Dr. Thompson continues. Next, he listens to Buddy's heart and lungs. "Sounds good." He gives his teeth and ears a cursory look. "Everything looks to be in good shape. He's what, about six or seven years old?"

I shrug. "I'm not certain. I've only had him since last year. We reckon he was abandoned. We took him to the shelter to check on his leg and for a chip or reports of a missing dog, but they didn't find either."

He pats Buddy's side. "He's a good boy. Lucky to have found a home." Rather than lift Buddy up to the table, Dr. Thompson sits on the floor and checks all his legs and hips, testing all his joints, and puts pressure on the leg in question. After a thorough examination of the paw and each paw pad, he shakes his head. "I don't see anything wrong. Nothing broken and there doesn't appear to be any swelling like we might find if he strained something. Nothing in his paw."

I pick up the leash and lead Buddy around the examination room. No limp. Not even a hesitation. "That's weird." I remember when he did this the day I found him. The next day that limp was gone too.

Dr. Thompson reaches in a glass container and pulls out a few dog cookies. "Maybe Buddy just wanted to visit us today, huh?" He dispenses the treats and rubs Buddy's neck. "If it happens again, give us a call, but I don't think there's any point in doing anything further today." He scribbles a note in the chart and hands it to Natasha.

"See you next time, Toby." He shakes my hand and tells Natasha to take the chart up to the front desk.

"Buddy's a beautiful dog," she says, leading the way to the front counter. "I can't imagine anyone abandoning him. I think it's great that you adopted him."

"Thanks. To be honest, I couldn't get rid of him if I wanted to." We laugh. "He waits for me after school in that same spot, unless it's baseball season, then he meets me at the field. I've never understood how he knows what to do."

"What a smart boy you are," she says, scrunching up her perfect nose and smiling at him.

While she talks to Buddy, my brain is in overdrive trying to think of a way to ask her out. I don't want to come off too forward, but can't let this moment slip by and then regret not saying something.

"Uh, since you're sort of new in town, would you like to meet up and grab a soda or ice cream some time?" I try to sound nonchalant, like it makes no difference to me.

"Sure, that sounds good." She turns her attention back to Buddy, whose tongue is hanging out as he laps up her affection. "Any guy that rescues you and take such good care of you has to be good, right?"

She studies the paperwork and moves behind the counter. "I could probably go tomorrow. How about we meet at the ice cream shop around two o'clock?" She retrieves my invoice from the printer and slides it over to me.

I let out the breath I had been holding. She said yes. I can't believe it. "That sounds great. I'll see you there."

She giggles and slides the bill closer to me. "How did you want to pay for this?"

"Oh, sorry." I pay for the visit and her eyes sweep to Buddy.

"You'd better bring Buddy with you."

"Don't worry, I can't go anywhere without him."

CHAPTER 14

I'm trying to pick out a shirt to wear to meet Natasha and Mom is fluttering in and out of my room, giving me her best advice. She's giddy with excitement about my "date" even though I tried to tell her it's not one. Just ice cream. But she insists on ironing the shirt I'm going to wear.

Although we get along better now, sometimes she still treats me like a little kid. Either she's overly involved in my life, like right now, or too busy with her students to notice me. It still bugs me that she and Dad are keeping something from me and think I'm incapable of handling whatever their secret is. I haven't found a good time to bring it up, but what if it's more serious? The more Mom looks for coupons and specials at the store, trying to convince me to pack my own lunch like she does, the more I worry she's struggling to stay afloat.

I've never been out with a girl by myself and I'm definitely more nervous than I thought I'd be. What if she asks a bunch of questions about my family?

It's in moments like these that a dad's advice could really help, and as Mom wanders off—likely to get the iron out again—I reach for my phone in the pocket of my jeans and look for his number in my contacts.

I could call him. I remember him telling me about the first time he met Mom. He was stationed at the local base and she worked at a place called the Penguin that served burgers and ice cream. He'd tell the story about placing individual orders for each of his buddies at the table just to have the opportunity to talk with Mom and wait at the counter. Mom would blush and they'd laugh. It was a happy memory and I could use a little advice. I scroll to his name and flick my thumb to connect the call, but can't press the button. With his unpredictability, I don't want to risk any complications right now. I'm nervous enough as it is.

At least Buddy will be there. I think he's the whole reason she's willing to meet me. He gives me a look that implies there is no doubt. I adjust my shirt once more, trying to keep the collar Mom insisted I wear from rubbing my neck. I check the mirror one more time and use my fingers and a dab of pomade to style the top of my hair where it's a little longer. "Let's go, Buddy."

Mom slips me a twenty dollar bill on my way to the van. "Have fun. I can't wait to hear all about her when you get home." She stands in the driveway and waves until I turn the corner.

I park on the side of the ice cream shop. The servers know Buddy from our visits and bring him a bowl of water and a dog treat while we wait at an outdoor table. It's a sunny day and the light sparkles as it dances on top of the lake. Buddy stands and cocks his ears minutes before Natasha comes around the corner. She's smiling and wearing a sweater the same intense blue of her eyes.

As she gets closer, Buddy's tail goes into hyper-drive and matches the pounding in my chest. I can't help but notice the swath Buddy's cutting with his tail, churning up bits of dirt from the sidewalk. He gets excited whenever Chet and Lyle are around, but this level of enthusiasm is usually reserved for me. She pets Buddy and talks to me even though she hasn't looked at me yet—maybe she's nervous too.

"Hi, Toby. How's it going?" I breathe in a hint of coconut. Just the sight of her makes my pulse quicken. I steady my voice and try to sound casual.

"It's all good. What have you been doing today?"

"Just getting ready for school tomorrow." She slides into her chair, continuing to rub Buddy's ears. "I've got all these new books I'm supposed to have read, and my stepmom won't stop asking me if I need help with them. I was happy to leave and get away for a couple of hours."

I take the chair next to hers. "Stepparents. I haven't even considered that dilemma. Makes me glad Mom doesn't date. I don't think she ever will."

She frowns and gives me a quizzical look. "I wouldn't count on that. It could happen, you know…"

I shudder and change the topic. The last thing I want to imagine is Mom dating some guy. "Your dad seems nice. Has he always been a vet?"

She nods. "Yeah, he's great and has been a vet since before I was born. He just works all the time. He promised to take more time off while I'm here these next couple of years." She shrugs. "We'll see."

"If you stay here with Buddy, I'll go in and get our ice cream. What do you want?"

She opts for the coffee fudge and I go inside to order. In addition to our ice cream, the lady at the counter gives me a tiny cup of frozen yogurt for Buddy. It seems all the ladies like him.

In between spoonfuls, we share bits about ourselves. With both of us having divorced parents, we commiserate over the dynamics of our situation but she seems to have a good relationship with her dad. "When I'm here in the summer, we are usually busy spending time at the lake or hiking. He cuts back on work and tries to spend as much time as possible with me. Now that I'll be living here, it will be different. Not like a fun vacation."

"With summer coming, it will be busier around here. I was surprised last year with all the tourists here for events at the lake." I accidentally bump her arm with my hand and she flinches, like I've hurt her. "Sorry, are you okay?" Buddy inches closer to her and rests his head atop her feet.

Her laugh is filled with nervousness and she studies her ice cream. "Oh, yeah, fine." She fingers the thin leather and silver bracelets on her wrist. "Summer is busier, but nothing like Denver or Seattle. The lake is always a popular attraction and loads of fun. The wineries do a ton of business and I guess the restaurants are busier, it just doesn't seem overwhelming to me."

"Well, it's nothing compared to a city, where it's always crowded." I glance at Buddy and find him still resting on Natasha's feet, his eyes closed.

She gets a far-off look in her eyes. "I like Riverside, I just miss some of the hustle and bustle and I really miss my favorite coffee shop. It was in an old warehouse space with lots of brick and tall windows. It had this amazing wall made out of wooden doors that had been refinished and painted bright colors and used beautiful second-hand chairs at the tables. They even had creative space in it for artists. I used to spend several hours a day there, doing homework and checking out the artwork."

"I'm not much of a coffee drinker." I tip my spoon of chocoholic in her direction. "More of an ice cream guy."

She laughs. "I love it. My high school even had a coffee bar in it. I'll have to make do with Lakeside Coffee." She scrunches her nose and moves her head in the direction of the coffee shop across the street.

"My mom is friends with the women who own Two Sisters and I know they have a bunch of fancy coffee drinks on their menu."

"Hmm, I'll have to check them out. I never knew they had coffees."

"Are you all set for your classes? Do you know your schedule?" She seems so relaxed and confident and it's all I can do to keep my tongue from getting tied in knots.

She moves a strand of hair behind her ear and shrugs. "I don't have my schedule, but am supposed to be transferring to the same level of classes I was in back home. I was hoping to stay in

Denver until the end of school, but it didn't work out. I'm stuck finishing these last few weeks here. I'm taking all the basics and for my electives I chose all art classes."

"Art again, huh? What type of art do you like?"

Her eyes brighten and light up her whole face. "I love to draw more than anything, but I do a bit of watercolor painting as well. I met a potter at the coffee shop and was thinking about giving that a try, but…"

"It's hard to let go of the familiar. I still miss my favorite Greek place, Niko's. There is no Greek food in Riverside."

She giggles and says, "Mexican food is the most exotic thing you'll find here."

We talk more about school and I tell her about my interest in engineering and that I'm researching colleges that might offer baseball scholarships. Buddy is now lying on the ground between our feet, having polished off his yogurt.

"You're lucky you know what you want to do. I'm not sure, but I know I want to do something related to art."

"You could go into advertising or marketing, lots of options. One of my friends back in Seattle, his older sister designs websites and logos," I say, reaching to pick up our empty bowls.

She shrugs. "I may not go to college right after graduation. I'm still not sure and I don't want to stress about it. Dad said I can work in the clinic as long as I like while I figure it out."

I wipe my sweaty palms on some napkins, thankful for the cool ice cream since my mouth feels like sandpaper. I've never felt like this before. I could listen to Natasha all day and there's something about her that makes me want to be near her.

Natasha's situation doesn't sound as volatile as mine. She seems to like both of her parents and has fun with her dad. I'm not sure I'm ready to share the level of dysfunction in our family. "I wasn't sure I'd like it here, being such a small town, but I like school here much better than I did in Seattle."

"You've got a great slider pitch. Did you play baseball there?"

I shake my head. Buddy stands and rests his head on Natasha's thigh, earning him a cuddle.

She winks at me and I notice how long her eyelashes are. "You're impressive for not having played before. Just a natural talent, huh?"

My cheeks redden with a mixture of embarrassment and pride at her words. "Coach has taught me so much about pitching. I think I just had a good throw and he helped me finesse it. Baseball is much more complicated than I ever realized."

"One more game until the championship, right?"

I nod, surprised at her knowledge. "Where'd you learn so much about baseball?"

She smiles and says, "When I was a kid, my, uh, we… I mean, my family went to all the local games." The smile is gone and sadness fills her eyes. She starts to rub her napkin between her fingers, shredding it into jagged strips. "So, just one more game, then?"

"Right. We'll be going to state, hopefully undefeated if things go our way next week. We have to travel for it, but I know they're organizing a couple of fan buses to attend the game."

She gives me a bright smile. "Everyone will be there, trust me. Riverside is obsessed with high school sports." She blushes and adds, "I'll be there for sure." She rubs Buddy's ears and looks at her watch. "Look, I'd better get going. My dad is picking me up at four sharp. Thanks for the ice cream."

Buddy and I walk her to the corner, where he chooses to stand next to her, and she gestures at a car coming down the street.

As we stand on the sidewalk, I wonder more about her. Despite her openness and what comes across as confidence, there's something else about her. I noticed how Buddy comforted her and stuck close to her. Maybe he sensed the same thing.

CHAPTER 15

As I'm getting on the bus Friday to travel over an hour north for our last game, I spot Natasha and wave. A wide grin fills her face as she returns the greeting, but as I watch her through the window walking from the building, she stops in front of Evan, who is leaning against the fence in the same spot he's always occupying. He's probably hassling her like he did me. Maybe he preys on all the new students. I hope he's not trying to ask her out.

More than a flicker of concern nags at me. I look at the open bus door and consider how long it would take me to run over there and intervene. I can't miss the bus, and I've been trying desperately not to react to Evan, but I hate seeing her subjected to whatever he's spewing.

"You've been texting that girl all weekend, do you have to stare at her now too?" Lyle jokes, sliding into the seat next to me and following my gaze. He's unzipping every pocket on his backpack in search of something, but my eyes never stray from the window. "How many pictures of Buddy do you plan to send her anyway?" He laughs, but I can't even reply—if I could just read lips. "It's hard to believe those two are brother and sister, isn't it?" Lyle says, dropping his backpack to the floor.

"Really?" I turn to look at him, and then straight back out of the window, searching my memories for Evan's last name. Thompson? I'm not sure.

I hadn't seen much of Natasha this week other than to say hello when we passed each other in the hallway, but apparently Lyle has been doing a bit more digging for me. His friendships with all the student ambassadors are finally benefitting me.

"You look like somebody just picked a homerun off you," says Lyle.

"Uh, yeah, I'm just shocked, I guess. They're so different and I never made the connection. She's never mentioned Evan."

"I wouldn't mention him either, if he was my brother." Lyle smirks. One of the guys taps him on the shoulder and Lyle holds up something from his bag. "I'll be right back," he says, following the guy to the back of the bus.

As the bus pulls away, my eyes are drawn to Natasha and Evan. She's still there, but standing more than a few steps away from him. He's talking and she's staring at the ground, hugging her books to her body. He moves his hands as he talks and takes a step toward her, but as the bus turns, they're no longer visible.

Evan's probably filled Natasha's head with plenty of his thoughts about me. As I think back to them standing there, the only feature they share is the color of their hair. She's petite and he's tall. She's kind and lovely and he's rude and arrogant. It would be my luck to fall for a girl with a brother who hates me.

I've thought about her all week. There's something mysterious about her, something I can't quite figure out, but I want to have a chance to get to know her better. Now, with Evan in the picture, I'm not sure I'll get it.

We get to the school and play their mediocre team, resulting in an easy win, which allows us to finish the year with an undefeated record. As soon as the game ends and we shake hands with all the players, Coach calls me over and introduces me to Mr. Bailey, who is a baseball scout.

I shake his hand. "Toby, I've had my eye on you for several games and you did not disappoint today," he says, his grip firm. "Have you given college much thought yet?"

"Yes, sir, I've been looking into colleges."

"Excellent. I've got a coach at Boise State that is interested in you. He'd like to meet you, have you visit for a few days, check out the campus, and the baseball program."

"That sounds great." I struggle to focus on what Mr. Bailey is saying, while in the back of my mind I'm trying to figure out how we can afford a trip to Boise.

Mr. Bailey touts all the amenities at Boise State and tells me there's also some interest from the University of Arizona in Tucson and Oregon State in Corvallis. "Coach Drumm at Boise is the most anxious and they're willing to foot the bill to get you over there for a visit."

Three schools? I can't quite believe it. To think I had no hope of going to college, to have three choices blows me away. As I wonder if they all have engineering programs and picture myself in a modern laboratory, a surge of excitement rushes through me. I feel like I'm flying with the thrill of this news, news that I still can't quite grasp is true. This means we could quit worrying about how to pay for college. I'd no longer have a financial connection to Dad, and neither would Mom. I can't wait to see Mom's face when I tell her the news. Did he say Boise will pay for the trip?

"So, what do you say, Toby? I can help make the arrangements for you and your Mom to visit as soon as championships are over. Will that work?"

"Uh, yeah, I think so. I'll need to talk to Mom tonight."

He hands me a folder emblazoned with the blue and orange colors of the Boise State Broncos. "My card is in there, as well as Coach Drumm's, with our cell phone numbers. If you have any questions, call either of us. We could shoot for the first week in June, after school's out?"

I bob my head in understanding, even though I'm overwhelmed with all the information. Coach Hobson steps forward and puts his arm around my shoulder. "I'd say Toby is surprised, to say the least. I'll make sure he and his mom understand

everything and we'll get back in touch with you in a few days."
He raises his brows at me. "Does that sound like a plan?"

"Sure, yes, thanks." I extend a hand to Mr. Bailey. "I appreciate
all this."

He shakes my hand again and then Coach's. "Talk to you soon.
Congratulations on the win today and a great season." He touches
his fingers to the bill of his ball cap and heads to the parking lot.

I stare at the back of the scout, an ordinary man of no significant stature, who looks more like a fan than someone involved
in choosing players for teams. I tap my feet on the ground and
pinch the inside of my arm to make sure I'm not dreaming. This
would change my life. How little I knew then that a small step
outside of my comfort zone would have the power to bring me
such an opportunity.

"You okay, Toby? You look like a deer caught in the headlights," Coach says as he guides me toward the locker room. "Get
your stuff and I'll meet you on the bus."

I hurry to the locker room, where Chet and Lyle are waiting
for me. "Where have you been?" asks Lyle.

"Coach wanted me to meet a baseball scout. He said Boise
State is interested in me." I hurry to stuff everything in my bag.

"That's great. A scout for Kansas State talked to me earlier
today." Chet grinned. "That's one of my top picks for a school."

"Is that the one with the agricultural program? Are you going
to go and visit?" I ask.

He nods with enthusiasm. "Yep. We're going to go for a few
days this summer." He turns to Lyle. "Are you still set on going
to Western Washington?"

Lyle bobs his head as we head outside. "Yeah, it makes the
most sense. I'm not as great a baseball player as either of you,
and I'm not cut out for a big city. Pullman isn't too far away and
they offer agriculture and business, which is what I'll need to
focus on to take over the farm. My dad did it without going to

college, but he wants me to go." His voice doesn't hold the same enthusiasm as Chet's.

"Have you been there to check it out?" I ask.

"Yeah, my older sister went there, so I've been there dozens of times."

I wonder if the choice was left up to Lyle alone, where he'd go, what he'd do.

As we turn the corner to head to the parking lot, Natasha waves at me. She's standing alone, waiting. I tell the guys I'll catch up with them and turn toward her.

She's decked out in the school colors, complete with green and gold ribbons in her hair. Her smile lifts her face, all the way to her eyes, sparkling with excitement. I quicken my pace, anxious to reach her and talk to her before the bus leaves.

"Hey, Toby. Great game. Congratulations on the win," she says.

"Thanks, I've been meaning to try to catch up with you at school, but this week has been hectic. Maybe we can meet for lunch one day next week?"

The impatient honk from a bus startles her and she looks over her shoulder. "I've got to run, or I'll miss my ride home. I'll text you and maybe we can get together this weekend?" She flashes me those gorgeous eyes but it still feels like there's something wrong.

"Sounds great," I say, hoping I'm reading too much into things. "Thanks for coming to the game," I holler as she runs to the bus.

I step onto our bus and Lyle gives me a discreet thumbs up, having watched my exchange with Natasha from his window, but all I can focus on is what Evan's been telling Natasha about me.

As I thumb through the packet of information from Boise State, I remember my interview at the local theater tomorrow. Ginny recommended me to the owner and it would be the perfect summer job. I printed out some generic interview questions I found online and intended to use my travel time to review them. I rummage in my backpack and pull out the questions and a pen. Lyle leans over and collects his backpack.

"You look busy, I'll be back in a sec."

I'm too excited to concentrate much, but I survey the list, most of which seem basic and straightforward, jot down a few answers and think about my strengths. I settle on hard-working and a good problem-solver for the attributes I want to make sure to convey during my interview.

What a perfect day. I never dreamed life in a small town could be this good.

CHAPTER 16

Parties aren't my thing. With countless birthdays and holidays interrupted by Dad's sudden departures, it never seemed too important to get swept up in the moment or get too excited, but I've got to be at the gazebo at five o'clock tonight for just such an occasion. The mayor is hosting a huge celebration to honor the baseball team for bringing home the championship trophy. Coach Hobson made it clear we'd all be there, even though school's out for the summer.

Natasha is going to meet me as soon as I get off work. Mom and I just got home last night and I haven't seen Natasha since we left for our visit to Boise State earlier this week. I'm dying to spend time with her and tell her about the trip.

We haven't been able to get together as much as I would like, with finals and the end of school and then Mom and I taking off for Boise. She still hasn't mentioned Evan and I'm not sure if that's good or bad. I wish I understood their relationship more, but keep hoping he hasn't poisoned her against me, and so far, so good. School got out right before Memorial Day and we spent one day hiking up in the hills with Buddy, picnicking with the view of the lake below us. Coach Hobson had a pool party at his house for the team on Memorial Day, and Natasha went with me. We even squeezed in a quick trip to the far end of the lake the day before I left for Boise and sat on the shoreline and watched Buddy swim and retrieve his toys. Despite texting all the time, being away from her these last few days, I've missed her.

There's not much to do at the theater while the customers are watching movies, so I've been reading to pass the time. The few times I've tried to read at home, Buddy pawed at the book until it fell to the floor, as if he was insisting we spent our time together playing outside. Mrs. Norman let me keep both books for the summer and though I've always avoided reading, the story about the astronaut stuck on Mars and his refusal to give up has captured my interest. My favorite part of the book was when he came up with that ingenious way to power the rover so he could travel across the surface of Mars to the old relic spacecraft and use it to send a message to NASA. It reminds me of the projects I'm working on in my engineering class.

I never thought reading a book could make me feel like I was right there inside the spacecraft, but it did. It would be so scary to be all alone and have to figure out how to survive, especially with such limited options. I check the clock, close the book, and stuff it into my bag.

Natasha's standing outside the entrance waiting for me. My heart flutters and I hesitate a beat, but slip my arm next to hers, clasp her hand in mine, and link our fingers together. My nerves tingle, unsure if my desire to feel her soft skin against mine and move closer to her will make her feel awkward. I search her face for a sign. She squeezes my hand and tilts her head up at me. The sparkle in her eyes and her wide smile reassure me that she feels the same. I've missed having her next to me while I was in Boise. When I'm with her everything seems enhanced—the sun is brighter, food tastes better, and the breeze is sweeter. It's something more than friendship I'm feeling.

We stroll down the sidewalk and I tell her how much I enjoyed visiting Boise State, describing the beautiful campus and their top-notch engineering program, along with the dorm I'd be assigned. "The Boise River runs right alongside the campus and the whole place is like a small town of its own. There's a motel close to campus, and Buddy will love it when he comes to visit; he can romp and run along the banks and play in the water. Mom and I both think it seems like the perfect fit for me and she likes that it's not too far from home." I take a deep breath and add, "Just don't want you to forget me." I laugh.

Natasha stops walking and focuses her eyes on mine. "Toby, this is a wonderful opportunity. I could never forget you. You won't lose me just because you're a few hours away." She winks and grins. "Are you set on going there?"

I nod. "With them offering a full ride, I'm set on it. I guess if another school comes up with the same offer, I'll have a decision to make, but right now, I'm planning on it."

"I'm so proud of you." She perches on her tiptoes and wraps her arms around my neck. I breathe in the scent of her and close my eyes as a comforting warmth travels through my body. I put my arms around her and know I could hold her like this forever.

We make our way to the gazebo, where people wearing team shirts are gathering for the mayor's presentation. Green and gold flags are strung across the street in a zigzag pattern, streamers and balloons decorate the town square and gazebo. The band is playing the school song and everyone is singing along, when I feel a tap on my shoulder. Mom is behind us, smiling with her phone out to capture photos. She bends her head close to Natasha's and the two of them chat and laugh with each other.

Mom and Natasha bonded when she came over to the house the day before we left for Boise. Mom was baking road trip snacks and she and Natasha chatted about their favorite recipes, with Natasha jumping in to help with the baking. She even offered to check on Buddy while we were away, since the activities at the college campus weren't conducive to four-legged students.

Despite the hours Mom and I spent in the van and her jabbering on about how lovely Natasha is, I didn't divulge how much I like her, or that over the past weeks my feelings for her have intensified. Being away from her while we were in Boise was rough. She's on my mind constantly and it seems like all I do is think of the next time we'll be together.

But I worry what will happen when she knows me better and finds out more about my family, especially my relationship with Dad and all the trouble I've been in. Will she look at me the same way she does now? What if she has to meet him? I don't want to keep things hidden from her, but I can't think of a way to tell her without the risk of losing her.

The mayor steps up to the microphone on the edge of the gazebo and welcomes the crowd. He invites the team to join him, along with the cheerleaders and our pygmy goat mascots. Chet and I end up standing next to each other in the front row as we pose for photos for the yearbook staff and the local newspaper.

I'm still in awe over the recognition the team received from the entire town. When our bus came back from Yakima after the win, we were met by fire trucks and police vehicles from Riverside. They escorted us all the way into town and the streets were lined with vehicles filled with residents and well-wishers honking their horns, cheering, and clapping. Being the object of all the adoration from the whole town was a bit unnerving, but the smiling faces of the people in the crowd, beaming with pride and cheering when the pennant and trophy were unveiled, told me it meant much more than a win—it's their sense of community.

Coach Hobson steps between Chet and me and says a few words to thank the community for their support, bestowing more praise on the team for our teamwork. The crowd cheers when he mentions our undefeated season. "I'm honored to be a small part of the lives of these incredible young men. They rose to the occasion and played a remarkable season and we ended the year with one of the highest grade point averages in the league. I'm proud to be their coach and teacher." He slips an arm around Chet and me.

The crowd is still cheering and waving pompoms when Mom makes me pose for photos with Chet and Lyle and Coach Hobson and takes several of me with Natasha.

She scans her phone and smiles, standing between Natasha and me. "These are terrific." She points across the street and says, "How about I treat you two to a celebratory coffee?" She raises her brows at me and adds, "Or smoothie?"

Natasha, always up for one of those fancy coffee drinks she likes, nods her head enthusiastically. Mom leads the way to Lakeside Coffee and claims one of the outside tables, handing me a twenty. "We'll get this table and you can order for us."

I join the end of a long line waiting to order. As I wind my way forward a few steps at a time, I'm perched in the corner, against the wall with the windows opened to the outdoor patio seating.

"I know issues like those are a real struggle. Toby's dad has been battling that since before we moved here."

Natasha murmurs something, but I can't make out what she says. The emotion in Mom's words is impossible to ignore. "William's doing better now, but his aggression and anger made it impossible to live with him and it's taken a toll on us. All of us."

I resist the urge to interrupt—I've never told Mom to keep things from Natasha but it's not her place to say anything. And what issues is she even referring to?

Memories of Dad swirl through my mind as I wait for our order, hurrying the barista along.

I pick up our order and as soon as I get to our table, Mom and Natasha quit talking. I hand Mom her latte with her change and place Natasha's caramel macchiato in front of her. I slip into my chair between them and hold my smoothie between my hands. Mom's joyful smile has been replaced with a serious expression and Natasha's eyes are puffy and red.

They paste on happy looks and take a sip of their drinks. I don't want to upset either of them, but I have so many questions. Why would they be discussing Dad at all? Mom breaks the silence and rambles on about how wonderful the ceremony was and how the whole downtown is bustling with excitement.

Every few minutes someone walks by and says congratulations and pats me on the shoulder. I smile and mumble my thanks, but on the inside, I can't relax. I take a sip of my smoothie and am immediately sorry. My stomach roils and I push the cup to the center of the table.

I stare at Mom, wondering what in the world she was thinking telling Natasha things about Dad, about our family, information that should be private. She's been keeping something from me all this time and then blurts it out to Natasha. The last thing I need is for Natasha to know something that could jeopardize what we have.

Mom looks at her watch and says, "I'm meeting Ginny and Molly for dinner. You two enjoy yourselves." She stands and squeezes my forearm. "Give me a call when you're ready to be picked up."

She gives us a little wave as she makes her way to the sidewalk. I toss Natasha's empty cup and my smoothie into the trash.

"Do you mind if we skip pizza and just take a walk down by the marina?"

"I need to leave earlier than I thought anyway, so a walk would be great," she says, taking my hand in a tight grip. I concentrate on the horizon and the sensation of Natasha's hand in mine, but immediately I know something has changed between us. It's a perfect early summer night, with the setting sun reflected in the calm water. The bushes that line the pathways are lit up with miniature white lights and the sweet scent of the blooming mock orange plants surrounding the space fills the air.

We're almost at the railing when Natasha's sandal catches on one of the cobblestones in the pathway and she starts to trip. I reach out and catch her. She turns her head to look up at me and her lips brush against my chin.

Her hands grip my back tighter and she makes no attempt to move away; in fact, she shifts closer to me, her eyes locked onto mine. Holding her close, with the trace of her breath on my lips, I feel an uncontrollable desire to kiss her. The urgency I feel to connect with Natasha is stronger than anything I've experienced—maybe she'll reject me, but my pulse quickens and I inch closer to her and meet her lips with mine.

Her lips are soft and gentle and I taste the subtle hint of caramel as I cover her mouth with mine. I shut my eyes and the world goes silent, save for the pounding of my heart fluttering in my chest. As the kiss deepens and her fingers dig into my shoulders, it's as if we're the only two people alive. The tropical scent of her hair mingles with the floral essence I detect along her neck. The sensation of her lips against mine and the delightful scent sends a tingle through me and makes my legs weak.

My mind goes blank and when we part, I look into her eyes, unsure if she feels the same elation I do. Her eyes sparkle in the twilight and her lips curve into a smile. I tilt my forehead into hers, immersing myself in her scent, before burying my mouth along the side of her neck, taking pleasure in the thrill of her soft skin against mine. She bends her neck back and her breath catches.

Every cell in my body is on high alert and I don't want this moment to end. How could I survive, even for a week, without this?

Soft footsteps on the pathway remind me we're not alone and I take Natasha's arm to move us out of the middle to allow the couple to pass by us. Natasha links her hand in mine and I get a warm and tingly sensation all through my body as we walk along the railing, and she rests her head against my arm.

CHAPTER 17

Mom is out running errands the next morning when the house phone rings. I don't pay attention to the number and when I answer it Dad's voice bellows from the receiver. He had called Mom's cell phone but didn't get an answer. He wants to know where she is.

Now I know he's dealing with something, I should try to be patient. I don't want to ask Mom about it—it would be absolutely pointless, but I take a breath and try to calm my nerves. I always respond to him quickly. Maybe I'm too brash. I should try a different tack.

"She's running errands. I'll tell her you called," I say. "How are you?" Maybe he'll tell me more about what's going on.

"Since I've got you and you never see fit to call me, your mom tells me your grades have improved and you're doing well in baseball," he says, instead of answering my question. "Sounds like you finally straightened up and listened to me about being responsible."

When I mess up it's my fault, but when I do well, it's due to his words of wisdom. Right. Buddy's tail thwacks into my leg.

I pet his head and take a deep breath. "Coach Hobson is a great teacher and coach. He's helped me learn to pitch and makes sure we all have help with our studies, if we need it. We had a great year."

"Is he a military man?"

Of course, if he's had a positive impact, he must be in the military. I resist a snarky tone. "I don't know, Dad, it's never actually come up in conversation."

"Tell your mother to call me when she gets home and you'd better keep on the right path, young man. Things can take a quick spiral downward if you slack off and lose your focus."

I draw in a long breath, choose not to respond, and tell Dad I'll relay his message and say goodbye. Just once I'd like to hear him encourage me, but that's never going to happen. Buddy is resting his head across my lap and looks up at me with his kind eyes. He's always there when I need reassurance or a sympathetic ear. He believes in me and trusts me, which in turn gives me confidence.

He takes off for the front door and I stomp over, flinging it open and find Natasha coming up the walkway. Her dad's car flips around in the street and he waves.

"What are you doing here?" As soon as the words leave my mouth, I realize how harsh they sound and the wary look on Natasha's face makes me wince. "Sorry, I didn't mean it like that. I'm just surprised to see you. Good surprised." I reach for her hand.

"You look upset, what's wrong?" She frowns and accepts my hand, her eyes clouded with worry.

"Oh, my dad called." I brush my lips against hers. "It's not important. I'm glad you stopped by." I shove my feelings about Dad to the back of my mind and drink in the sight of Natasha, holding her hands in mine. Just being next to her calms me and makes me feel at ease.

"Your mom called me and said she got a bunch of fresh strawberries and invited me over to make jam. I've never made it and wanted to learn." Buddy nudges his nose against her leg and she bends to oblige him with a pat on the head.

Buddy escorts us back into the house and urges us into the backyard, where I keep a bunch of balls for playing catch. Natasha and I sit on the patio and I toss balls to Buddy, who retrieves each one and begs for another throw. "So, what's going on with your dad? You never say much about him, but it helped your Mom to talk the other night." She speaks quietly as I throw another ball to the far end of the yard.

I take a deep breath as I weigh my options. I knew I'd have to tell her more about our family, but have never found the right time. I could keep things to myself, but what if I lose her? I look into her eyes, reassured by the love and kindness in them. I only hope what I'm about to tell her won't change her feelings about me.

"He called to talk to Mom, but had to go into his father-of-the-year lecture mode." I shake my head with disgust. "He's in the military and hasn't been around much in the last several years. Long ago, when I was little, I have memories of us being a normal family, but things haven't been good for a long time." She takes my hand in hers and nods, as if she understands.

I clasp her hand for just a second before I drop it, and keep tossing balls, hoping she won't notice how nervous I am. "Things got worse, with him being gone even more and when he was home, he was angry all the time. I didn't want to be around him and all he did was bark orders at us. Our family dissolved in front of me. Dad left, they got divorced, and we had to move here and our relationship hasn't gotten better; in fact, it's probably worse. I don't talk to him much and when we do talk, he's still barking orders at me and never really talking or asking about what's happening in my life. I have almost no connection to him."

Her eyes urge me to continue, as does the slight squeeze she applies to my hand. "Dad's not the only one with issues." I take a deep breath. I can't blame everything on him. "I've gotten into my share of trouble in Seattle. I felt angry all the time and would fly off the handle, getting into a few shoving matches and verbal scuffles at school. I was in detention all the time, didn't do my work, got horrible grades, and hung out with kids Mom said were bad influences."

I stare at the concrete, afraid to look at Natasha in fear of the disappointment I expect in her eyes. Despite the knot of apprehension in my stomach, I know I have to finish the story. "I ended up skipping school and going downtown with these friends. They were vandalizing stuff. I knew it was wrong, but I didn't want to be teased or mocked, so I was there egging them on, laughing as they tormented people. It was so stupid. I'm not even sure why I did it. Turns out security cameras captured all of our activities. That's the only thing that saved me from a bigger problem, since I didn't actually break the law, except for being truant. The school counselor at my mom's school talked to my counselor. Between the two of them and Mom, they were able to keep me out of the system, but it was way too close for her. And me."

I look up, embarrassment flushing my cheeks.

"Everyone screws up. You don't seem like that kind of a person now." Her hand rests on my knee.

"I got caught up in the moment."

Hoping to gauge her level of disapproval, I steal a glance at her. "The worst part though, before this happened, when Dad was home one weekend, we got in a huge fight. He was giving me another Alpha Charlie, as he calls an ass-chewing, and I'd had enough. He wouldn't shut up and just kept telling me how worthless I was and how disappointed he was in me and I punched him… in the face."

She sucks in a breath and her eyes go wide, but she doesn't let go of my hand.

"I've never punched anyone like that before, but it was the only thing I could think to do. I felt cornered and out of options. Talking to him never works. He just barks louder and never stops. I didn't even think, I just reacted with my fist, and then I ran. I didn't come home until Mom promised he was gone. He went back to work and I haven't seen him, in person, since." Tears burn my eyes and I pick up the ball Buddy just retrieved and walk out into the yard, hoping Natasha won't notice.

I focus on Buddy while I steal a few looks at Natasha. She's drumming her fingers on the table and concentrating on the flowers along the fence. Despite my fear that she'll dump me and not want anything to do with me, the heavy burden I've been carrying is gone. I've been avoiding this for so long.

After a few more throws to Buddy, I calm down and return to my chair next to Natasha. "He hurts me more than I can admit and I lashed out that day. That's how he was earlier. Not telling me he's proud of me for doing well in school or baseball, but making it all about him. It's been so long since we've had a normal conversation." I look at her and add, "I hope this doesn't change how you feel about me." My voice begins to crack and I don't trust myself to say anything else.

She takes my hand in hers and rewards me with a heartfelt smile, one that makes the corners of her eyes scrunch up a little. "Nothing could make me change how I feel about you. I'm sorry, Toby. I didn't realize how much you've been through. Trust me, I know families aren't always easy and have watched similar things unfold in our house. It sounds like your dad may be struggling, too."

Tears begin to sting my eyes, but I don't run away this time. "I'm ashamed that I hit him. It was horrible and I never should have done that, but I'm always the one he blames." Buddy plops the ball at my feet and presses his nose to my knee, offering comfort with his gentle eyes.

Sadness clouds Natasha's face. "Hitting him was wrong, no question. I can't believe he's never talked to you about it. Maybe someday you can have a conversation about all of it and explain how he made you feel." She shakes her head and sighs. "I struggled a little when my parents divorced. I knew they hadn't been getting along well, nothing explosive," she says quickly, looking at me briefly, then back to her hands. "But their relationship had dissolved into one that seemed apathetic, like neither one of them cared anymore. I was shocked when they told us they were getting divorced and wasn't happy that Dad would be moving so far away and I wouldn't get to see him often. I was embarrassed and didn't want my friends to know what had happened but I mostly missed my dad… so sometimes I resented being with my mom and was spiteful. I'd ignore her, volunteer her for things at school and not tell her so she'd look like a failure, lots of passive-aggressive stuff like that." She grimaced and said, "She needed help around the house and I wasn't there for her. I'm not proud of those things either. I was angry and blamed her for the situation."

She runs her hands over Buddy's back and he rolls over seeking a belly rub. "We eventually worked through it and I adjusted to our new normal, but it took some time. Now with this latest change, I didn't get to finish the year in Denver, which really made me mad, but you've got to look at the positives sometimes. I like being here and working with Dad. I've missed him and it's fun to be around him every day instead of just on vacation. I like working at the clinic, when I can have him all to myself, without my stepmom around. Part of me, that part that missed Dad for all those years, is glad Mom's job changed and I had to move here. Not to mention, I would have never met you." She winks at me and I release the breath I was holding.

I pick up the ball and toss it for Buddy. The way she accepted my admissions, without judging me and making me feel worse, makes me realize how special she is. Maybe her situation with her parents helps her understand mine. We might have more in common than I thought. It sounds like she harbored some resentment toward her mom, which she handled better than I did, but at least she can empathize with what I went through. "Buddy and I are certainly glad you're here, working at your dad's office."

Buddy's ears perk at the mention of his name and he hurries to us, drops his ball, and leans against Natasha.

She giggles and ruffles his neck. "I don't mind the clinic and I love animals, so it's the right place for me. You know, I used to fantasize that Mom and Dad would get back together and life would be normal again." I know how that feels. I've thought about having my perfect family back together more than I'd care to admit. "I think I went through a grieving period and it took some time. I can tell both of them are happier now."

"Our life is better without my dad. My mom is way happier and more relaxed, like a heavy weight has been lifted and she's free. She's finally doing things and going places with friends. He was like a constant dark cloud hanging over us, even when he wasn't home." Buddy nudges the ball to me, urging me to toss it again.

"I'm glad you and Buddy are here and it's nice that you and your mom are happier now."

"We are, but," I pause, not sure how much more I should tell her, "there's still something they're not telling me. Mom and Dad talk more often than I think is necessary and I've overheard her side of the conversation. She thinks I don't need to be burdened with something. I'm not sure what they're talking about, but always suspected it was our finances. Now, I think it could be something else."

"My mom and dad have money and they still argue about financial stuff, so you're probably right." Despite my tempting her, she isn't going to divulge what Mom told her at the coffee shop.

Buddy's snout raises in the air and he runs to the house. "Mom must be home," I say. "I swear he hears her van when it makes the turn into the subdivision. He always greets her."

Natasha meets her at the garage door and helps her tote in the buckets of fresh berries and canning jars, both of them smiling and chatting as they discuss the jam making process.

I pat Buddy's head as we watch the activity from the sliding glass door. I feel a closeness to Natasha I've never felt before with anyone. I smile as I watch her with Mom, listening to their happy chitchat. But I can't help wondering if she's keeping something from me.

CHAPTER 18

Now

I have a confession to make. I'm a bit of a romantic. There's nothing sweeter than those first sparks of interest. It's like the beginning of spring, when everything is new again: the bright green shoots and cheerful colors of the first blooms light up and breathe new life into the earth. That's what Natasha did for Toby.

There are so many different types of love. For instance, I love playing ball and I love chicken and I love Toby. I love all those things, but not to the same degree and not in the same way. The love for a person, especially a soulmate, is beautiful and special. Toby was my soulmate. But I might not have been his.

Love is full of wonder and euphoria, excitement and nervousness. It was clear Toby liked Natasha when he saw her that first time after the game. I smelled the pheromones and saw the spark in his eye.

Love begins with trust and when Toby opened himself up to Natasha and shared the side of him he wanted to keep hidden, I knew he was serious. Sensing her caring soul and watching her as she reassured Toby made my heart swell.

Love changes people, softens them. Even the most hardened hearts will yield. I watched as Toby's fears and anxiety dissolved and his heart opened to Natasha.

Love forces humans to be vulnerable, to share their deepest fears and secrets with someone new. In the process, the bond between the couple strengthens, as there is a power and intimacy in this shared knowledge. The world is less scary with a partner by your side.

Toby's lack of self-worth began to dissolve as our friendship endured. His life in Riverside transformed Toby from the burden-laden boy I first met, to a young man looking forward to tomorrow, but no one had as great an effect on him as Natasha.

I know my companionship made Toby stronger, but meeting Natasha amplified that. Not only was she a friend, but she held the allure, the promise, the mystery of so much more. As their infatuation with each other grew, I was privileged to have a front row seat to watch their love deepen.

She carried her own regrets and sorrow. I think there's a certain level of dysfunction in all families, but Toby felt he was alone in that circumstance, until she shared her own struggles with him.

I knew Toby was nervous about his budding relationship, but as in baseball, it's important not to let the fear of striking out keep you from playing the game. I sensed his relief when Toby realized she would accept him, blemishes and all, and together they began to grow closer, feeling as if the other completed each of them. Toby found love in baseball, Natasha, and me, albeit in different forms. Instead of being mired in despair and negativity, love gave Toby hope.

The power of love is well known, written about in songs and poetry, but to experience it is indescribable.

Humans and dogs crave love. It's like air and water. It's why Toby needed Natasha and it's what keeps me waiting for Toby today. There is a physical drive, not just an emotional one, to be connected, to belong. We all want to know we're not alone in the world.

It gave me such comfort to know that I wasn't all Toby had and I didn't have to be his whole world. Toby was so lonely when I met him, but in a short space of time he gained a lot of people he could rely on when he just opened himself up to the possibilities.

Because dogs don't have as long a lifespan as humans, I took comfort in the fact that Toby would have that love and support from someone else. He'd let himself trust someone, and he could do it again, if he needed to.

CHAPTER 19

Then

Natasha and I have so much fun together but I just can't shake this feeling in the back of my mind that she's keeping something from me. Whatever Mom said, perhaps she swore her to secrecy. And I know what it's like when Mom asks for your trust.

When I was young, Mom always let me help her wrap presents for Christmas. We'd pick out special treats and goofy toys to put in Dad's stocking and if he wasn't able to be home, ship it along with his gifts. She always made me promise to keep it a secret and explained the importance of her trusting me with secrets. One year, Dad was home for the holidays and while Mom was out running errands, I told him what was in every one of his wrapped boxes and listed all the funny things we put in his stocking. He thought it was hilarious, but Mom was furious that I had ruined the surprise and taken all the excitement out of Christmas morning. She refused to let me help her with wrapping after that year. Mom never involved Dad in her Christmas secrets, but whatever she said to Natasha involves him too. Is she trying to protect me?

It just hurts that they don't trust me and it scares me that I could be the reason for it.

Buddy and I are in the habit of walking to town each morning and he's sitting beside my bed, staring at me with his expressive eyes, telling me his patience is wearing thin and it's time we hit the road. We pass by the lush green fields, now tall with alfalfa and wheat. We can still play in the one small pasture that's used for grazing, when it's not full of sheep or cows.

I love the longer days of summer and the freedom to spend time playing catch with Buddy, along with the opportunity to keep my pitching skills honed. After dozens of throws and enthusiastic retrieves by Buddy, we continue down the road to town. The fruit trees in the orchard are crowded with still ripening apples and the bushes are heavy with berries. The loud buzz of bees working at the berry farm competes with the chirping of birds darting among the bushes and trees, hoping for a nibble. The blueberries are some of the first to ripen and as we walk by the fence, I snag a few from the long shoots that arch over the barrier. Buddy sits, waiting for his share. I savor the sweetness of them as we continue down the road.

I'd never had fresh berries right from the bush until we moved here. Mom's strawberry jam she made with Natasha is so good and Natasha made a to-die-for strawberry pie. They are so much sweeter and juicier than the ones we find at Sunshine Market. Natasha and I already made plans to go to the berry farm in August to pick raspberries and blackberries. She's got her eye on a prize during the upcoming Apple Festival in September and has been perfecting her recipes for apple-themed treats.

We pass by another fruit orchard that is busy with trucks coming and going as they're in the midst of harvesting their cherry trees. We reach the turn in the road and I marvel at the massive bigleaf maple, now adorned with its huge green leaves creating a canopy of shade that encompasses at least fifty feet. Buddy slurps up some water from the stream and I take a long guzzle from my water bottle before we dart under the tree and rest for a few minutes. The temperature under the tree is perfect and as I lean against its hefty trunk with Buddy's head resting in my lap, I know I could take a nap. Buddy's eyes are already closed.

This place, under this tree, is the place where I am most at ease. I never imagined I would enjoy sitting under a tree on a quiet country road. I'm not sure I ever sat under a tree back in Seattle. There weren't many places that were quiet like this, save for a park, but it was hard to find one of those that wasn't overrun with people. This is the perfect spot to think and relax, while taking in the beauty of the valley. In the bustle of the city and the hurried pace, I never paid much attention to trees and flowers, but here it's different. There's time to think and time to notice the subtle beauty of each season.

Natasha is waiting at our usual lunch spot when we get there, waving at us as we cross the street. Buddy makes a beeline for her and she rewards him with cuddles and ear scratches. I place our order inside at the counter and as I pull out my wallet, am thankful for the job at the theater. Having a little bit of spending money makes me less reliant on Mom, especially when I know money is tight. The two-for-one coupons are getting tiresome.

As I slide into my chair, I notice Natasha's usual smile is missing. I reach for her hand. "Are you okay? What's wrong?"

"Evan, my brother, and I had another argument. I just can't figure him out. One minute he acts like he wants to hang out with me and the next he's screaming at me. It seems like when he's not arguing with me, he's sullen and withdrawn. I was hoping we would reconnect now that I'm here and it would be more like it was when we were kids. I'm sure my arrival in Riverside disrupted his routine, but I thought he'd adapt and be more excited to have me here."

What I sensed she was keeping from me are her problems with Evan—nothing to do with my dad. I've been reluctant to say anything about Evan: since we didn't get along well after our first encounter, we've managed to avoid each other ever since—simply passing each other in the corridor. She explains that when her parents divorced, her mom couldn't handle Evan.

He was beginning to act out and was disrespectful, so her parents came up with the idea of each of them taking a child. "It sounds like a crazy arrangement, but when I think back to how Evan was acting and Mom in tears almost every day, I can understand it. I know there were times she was afraid of him. She's petite and there's no way she could control him physically, and he had no regard for her. At least he didn't walk all over my dad and still had a little respect for him. He basically ignored Mom and whatever she said."

"So you guys had been separated for several years before you came here? You'd only see him in the summer?"

She shakes her head and says, "No, that's when he goes to spend some time with Mom. So I never saw him at all. They seemed to be able to get along in limited doses and she usually planned something fun or took him on a trip, so that made things easier."

With a wistful look, she pokes at her taco. "When we were growing up it was different. He was my best friend, my protector. Being so close in age, we spent all our time with each other." She smiles and adds, "We had our share of squabbles, but they were resolved over popsicles or cookies."

"I've always wanted siblings." I smile, thinking they can get things back on track.

She takes another bite and nods. "I was never lonely and Evan and I always found something to do. We built forts in the yard and even had a treehouse where we'd hide from Mom and Dad. We shared our deepest secrets. We played game after game of cribbage." Tears cloud her eyes. "I miss the Evan I used to know. I miss my brother."

She frowns and adds, "I guess our parents should have figured out a way to schedule things so we could spend time with each other. Our relationships had begun to suffer when Evan started junior high. Once he and Dad left though, things got worse between us. When Mom and Dad first split, Evan and I used to talk to each other every week, but as time went by, his interest waned and I was busy with my own life and pushed him to the back of my mind. When I was here in the summer, I was just happy to have Dad all to myself."

She crosses her arms. "I was hoping he'd changed by now. He's beyond rude to our stepmother. He acts like he's in charge of me, telling me when I should be home, and always wants to know where I'm going. I think he's miffed that I'm living with them now. He's had all of Dad's attention and now has to share it with me."

She traces the grout line of the tiled table with her finger. "Dad has about had it with him. Their biggest fight now is over college. Dad wants him to go and Evan is being his usual uncooperative self. Dad is almost at the end of his tether and he's a patient guy. Dad makes a good living and never made Evan work. He thinks that was a mistake, which is why I have to work at the clinic." She clears her throat and laughs. "I haven't mentioned to Evan that Dad told me I could work there until I decided about college. That would start World War Three."

As I eat my second taco, I think about how I was acting back in Seattle. It sounds a little bit like Evan. From my few encounters with Evan, I can understand how he would be hard to handle at home, especially if he was determined to be uncooperative. I hope Dr. Thompson and Evan can figure things out before it results in something like what happened with me and Dad. Sometimes it takes something serious, like punching your dad in the face, to force a change. But I don't quite want to say that to Natasha.

"Evan and I didn't hit it off when I first moved here."

Her hands clench as one brow raises. "He doesn't hit it off with most people. He's angry all the time and unless you idolize him, he wants nothing to do with you. I'm willing to do anything to get him back. That's why I left early the night of the celebration at the gazebo. Evan agreed to a family dinner, but then after I got home, he wouldn't come out of his room. I can't figure out what to do. It's like I don't even know him anymore."

I examine the sidewalk for cracks. "I know what it's like feeling that sort of anguish, having anger and worry inside you that comes out in all the worst ways. I've lost my dad because of it and haven't found a path to mend our relationship, but we'll find a way. We both will."

Her eyes broaden and she puts her hand on top of mine, and I note the spark of electricity between us, the warmth of her hand, her delicate fingers, they feel so soft against my skin. "I'm sorry, Toby. I'm sure that's not easy for you." She smiles and my chest flutters. "You never seem angry. That's one of the things I like about you so much." She sighs and adds, "Evan has battled with his emotions since junior high. He was like that before the divorce directed most of his hatred toward Mom, but then seemed to get worse living with Dad. They still don't get along well and Evan does his best to avoid any family activities. I think Dad has given up and he doesn't force him to join in anything." She's fiddling with the hem of her dress, studying the brick wall beside her, and I can tell there's more to this.

Her laughter today seems forced and when I look at her plate, she's only managed to eat half of one taco. I sense her despair over Evan and would like to know more, but don't want to push it and upset her further. "I hate seeing you so sad about Evan," I say.

She purses her lips. "It's just been a bad day. I'll be fine."

"Could your stepmom help?"

Her eyes widen and she shakes her head. "No, I don't want to go there. I have a hard enough time convincing her I don't want to be her best friend."

"What about one of your girlfriends?" I haven't met many of Natasha's friends, but it is quite hard for me to focus on anyone but her.

She shrugs. "I don't really have a girlfriend here. It's not something I want people to know anyway." She moves her hand to grip mine. "You're my best friend, Toby."

Buddy puts a paw on her thigh and it's as if we're all linked together. She laughs and pats his head, which earns her a lick.

Fortunately for Natasha, I think I've got a plan.

I know what it's like to struggle with something and I'm sure a day on the water can help Natasha patch things up with Evan. When she shared how much she and Evan loved the lake and her happy memories, she told me about her dad's boat. Since then, he and I have been planning the day out—where we'll go, how we'll get Evan there. I just hope it all works out.

It's the annual Boat Poker Run and a beautiful mid-July day, the sun blazing in the morning sky with no breeze and the town is buzzing with activity. Mom offers to drop us off at the marina on her way to meet Ginny and Molly for a day of craft shows at the local wineries.

Buddy and I have spent some time at the lake. The water draws him like a magnet and I usually have to drag him out by the collar. We've spent many hours playing along the shoreline with his toys that float, but we've never been to the marina. Unless you're a member, there's a parking charge, and since we don't have a boat, we've never ventured beyond the gate.

As Buddy and I make our way to the dock, keeping an eye out for signage that will direct us to the slip number Natasha gave me, we approach the shoreline and Buddy can't help himself. He runs into the water and before I know it, he's submerged, with only his head bobbing along the top of the water as he swims a few feet out from the beach.

I don't want to be late, but can't resist letting Buddy have his fun. He paddles a bit and then lets the current carry him to the shore before he turns around and dives in again. In the midst of laughing at my goof of a dog, I feel a tap on my shoulder.

Natasha's dimples greet me. "I thought I'd start walking this way to meet you guys and spied Buddy in the water."

Buddy emerges from the shoreline and waits until he's next to us to shake and launch all the water from his fur onto us, with the result being he's dry and we're soaking wet. Natasha squeals with delight and says, "We've got a bunch of towels on the boat. Come on, we'll dry off."

As we meander from the sandy beach with Buddy trotting ahead of us, she grabs my hand in hers. "I'm so glad you're here." She pauses and adds, "Dad told me what you tried to do, but Evan decided not to come."

"How come?" I ask, afraid I already know the answer.

She grits her teeth. "He changed his mind. I baked batches of his favorite cookies," she holds up three fingers on her hand as her shoulders slump, "three different kinds. Dad told Evan he wanted him to captain the boat this year and show you how it was done. I thought we could play a game of cribbage and teach you while we had lunch. Evan seemed excited about the whole thing all week, but this morning it was a different story. We left him sleeping in his bed." Tears cloud her eyes and she adds, "I'm sorry, but I'm too tired to make up an excuse for him today."

I put my arm around her shoulders. "I'm the one who's sorry. This should be your day with your family and I tried to set something up. He probably felt pressured. Buddy and I can get a ride home and you can call Evan. It's probably me he doesn't want to see." I knew I should have arranged something that I wouldn't be present for.

She shakes her head. "No, I offered to stay home with him, but Dad says we can't let Evan control our entire life." Her lips curve, but it's not her usual smile that reaches all the way to her eyes. "We'll have a fun day, I promise."

We continue to follow the wooden dock pathways until we get in the right section of the marina. The further we travel, the more we're amid larger boats, much grander than the fishing boat Dad borrowed for our trip.

Natasha points at the slip and guides me to the deck at the rear of the boat. Buddy, who is now dry, follows us onto the boat. My shorts and shirt are still wet and I drip onto the boat with complete embarrassment. Dr. Thompson welcomes me and introduces me to his wife, Mandy, who comes over with a beach towel in her arms, and shows me where I can find a life jacket for me and a canine one for Buddy.

Natasha shows us around the fancy cruiser, pointing out the cabin below with a modest kitchen, table, and couches, plus a bedroom and bathroom. It's way bigger than I imagined.

We go back up to the deck and sit on the comfy cushioned seating area, while Dr. Thompson finishes his checklist. Mandy hands us each a plate and tells us to help ourselves to breakfast burritos and fruit.

Natasha may be struggling with Evan, but she's at ease with her dad, so I figure it may still be possible to give her a sense of family today.

Dr. Thompson shows us the map of the lake and the check-points and explains that we have to pick up a playing card at each checkpoint and then return to the Maple Lake Boat Club where the team with the highest poker hand wins a prize. There is also a prize for the first team to return to the club with all five cards, but he wants to enjoy the day on the lake and not rush.

"They're about to start." Natasha's dad makes for the cockpit and motions me to follow.

Buddy is content to sit by Natasha and get his ears massaged. I watch as Natasha's dad guides the boat out of the marina and out onto the lake. He points at the map and shows me the checkpoint furthest from our position. The cockpit sports a large windshield in front and is protected by a hardtop overhead with a sunroof, which is open. We increase our speed and traverse the water creating a strong breeze that ruffles through my hair. As we head further to the midpoint of the lake, Dr. Thompson turns to me and asks if I want to steer.

He slides out of the oversized leather chair and gestures for me to sit down. He gives me a reassuring nod, rests his knee next to me, and points at the shoreline ahead of us. "I'll be right here, just use a gentle touch and guide her toward the dock in the distance."

My heart quickens as I take the wheel and hold it steady. He explains the throttle and says, "I'll tell you when to slow it down as we get closer. I like heading this way first. Since most of the others set out to the first checkpoint, it's less crowded out here."

I relax as we continue and with only a few boats in this area, there's no traffic to navigate. With Dr. Thompson's help, I guide the boat alongside the dock. One of the men sitting on the dock brings over a hat and Natasha picks our first card—an unimpressive eight of diamonds.

We wave goodbye to the enthusiastic dock sitters, many of whom shout out to Dr. Thompson by name. As he settles into the captain's chair and Natasha and Mandy stretch out on the cushioned seats, I realize this is a perfect family day, one that should include everyone in their family. "I'm sorry I'm the reason Evan isn't with you today. I'm having such a good time, but hate to cause a problem with him," I say, pulling Dr Thompson aside.

He clasps my shoulder and says, "It's not you, Toby. I'm glad you're here. Evan could have come and enjoyed himself. I'm not going to worry about it and neither should you. This is not the first time Evan has skipped a family event, and I'm sure it won't be the last." A hint of regret lingers in his words.

I can't imagine not wanting to spend a day like today. With a sympathetic nod, I say, "Thank you, sir."

"You can call me Steve, we're not at the clinic today." He smiles and motions me to take over the boat.

We travel from point to point, collecting playing cards and a few homemade goodies from the dock owners, lunch on burgers Steve grills on the barbeque built into the upper deck of the boat, and return to the boat club in the late afternoon.

Despite not having a winning hand and leaving with a prize, Steve is cheerful and talkative as we work together to unload the supplies from the boat and cart them to his big SUV.

Natasha grabs her backpack and gives her dad a hug goodbye as he finishes battening down the boat, which I notice is named *Dock Holiday*. Clever and fitting for a doctor. We hold hands as we navigate the circular road and parking area, teeming with moving vehicles. Buddy stays right next to my leg and stops whenever I stop. I never have to worry about him darting ahead or taking off on his own.

"I'm so glad you came with us today. It was fun to have you there," she says, squeezing my hand. "I appreciate you trying to get Evan to enjoy a day on the lake with us. It means a lot to me, to Dad. I'm just sorry he didn't come."

"I wish he had, too." I spot Mom's van pulling to the side of the road. We hurry to meet her and climb into the rear seat.

"How was your day on the lake?" she asks.

"Incredible," I say, and we recount our water adventure on the drive home and show her a few of the pictures we captured from the boat.

Natasha and Mom have plans to audition a few new recipes for the baking contest. When we walk through the door, Mom's cell phone rings and she excuses herself to her room.

While I get some cold drinks from the refrigerator, Natasha pulls a wrapped box from her backpack. "I made you something," she says with her signature smile.

I untie the ribbon and open the box to reveal a framed drawing. It's of Buddy at the baseball field. "Wow, this is incredible." I marvel at the detail.

Her eyes sparkle at the compliment. "I told you I like art. I've been taking lots of photos of Buddy and then sketched this and colored it with pencils. It's not that involved."

I wink. "Maybe not for you. I could never do something like this in a million years." I stare at the drawing and then at Buddy, getting him to sit properly and act seriously like the picture. "I can't believe how lifelike it looks. I love it." I motion for her to follow me. "I've got the perfect spot for this on my bookshelf." I adjust the frame so the light hits it and enhances the drawing. "Buddy's eyes look so real, like they're actually shiny."

Natasha leans closer to me and her fingers follow the curve of Buddy's head. "I love drawing animals and he has such a kind expression in his eyes, I wanted to capture it."

I point at Buddy's ears and the little tufts of fur that stick out at the top where they meet his head.

She beams at me and then reaches to touch Buddy's ears. "I've stroked this guy's ears so many times, I drew most of him from memory." My head bobs in agreement, appreciating how spending time with someone enhances your ability to imagine them even when they're not there. I visualize the curve of Natasha's cheek, her deep dimples, and her gorgeous eyes when I shut my eyes each night.

She explains how she used different tones of the same color to add depth to his fur, making it look so realistic. "I had to study the variation in the colors of his coat. It's complex with so many shades of gold, along with hints of copper and red, and that almost white undercoat." The passion for her work is undeniable, revealed in her excited voice as she explains the details.

"I'll treasure it always," I tell her and wrap my arms around her. Buddy presses his nose to her leg and swishes his tail in obvious admiration of his likeness.

Mom's laughter floats from her room, where she is still on the phone. I roll my eyes and say, "It's got to be Molly or Ginny. She could be awhile."

"I'm going to get started on our project," says Natasha, leading me down the hallway. She retrieves her backpack and takes it into the kitchen.

I catch a glint of a reflection from the window and look out to see Evan's car at the curb. I open the door to invite him in and notice the frown on his face.

"I'm here to pick up Natasha. Where is she?" he barks. No greeting, no niceties, just that clipped sentence in a rough tone, and he stares at me with harsh eyes and a scowl. Despite his casual appearance, his crinkled shorts and smudged tank top, he doesn't appear to be relaxed. He's tapping his foot against the step, his impatience on full display.

I turn and look for her and feel Buddy against my leg. A few seconds later she comes around the corner, wearing her apron and a look of confusion. "Evan, what are you doing here?" she says.

"Dad told me to come and get you. Get your stuff."

Natasha looks confused, her brow furrowing slightly. "Toby's mom is going to drop me home later tonight. Dad knows that. I've only been here—" Buddy steps over to Natasha and sits in front of her.

"Don't argue," he interrupts. "Change of plans. Get your stuff and get a move on." He motions to his car parked at the curb, a silver sedan, which looks like an older model of the car Natasha's dad drives—a hand-me-down.

"OK." She shakes her head, embarrassment flushing her cheeks. "I'm sorry about not cleaning up my mess, Toby. I really should get back anyway." I know exactly the kind of influence

Evan is having on her, but after he's missed out on this entire day, maybe they need some time together.

Evan ignores her, sneers at me, and glares at Buddy.

Natasha hurries to the door and apologizes again, following Evan to his car. He guns the engine as he pulls away and speeds down our street.

Mom raises her eyebrows as she comes to the door. "What was that?"

"Evan picked Natasha up, I think she got her wires crossed."

I know Mom's not convinced, but it's better this way. Natasha knows Evan the best and I've got to trust her. Something about this worries me, though, but I've got to control my anger too.

CHAPTER 20

You know that feeling you get in your gut when you know something isn't right? I felt it that morning when I listened to Dad on the staircase before we moved here, I used to feel it on the way home when I knew I'd find Mom crying, and I should have listened to myself when it happened that Saturday before school started.

Though we've been enjoying our time at the lake, including dinners at the Maple Lake Boat Club, courtesy of Natasha's dad, berry picking with Buddy on the walking trail that loops around the lake, and a movie in the park one night—*To Kill a Mockingbird*—I feel like Natasha is holding something back from me. She never told me what she and Evan did when they left that day. If they spent any time together or talked at all, and their relationship seems more strained than ever.

My bookshelves are now filled with more drawings from Natasha, several of me with Buddy and one of me pitching at the championship game. Instead of my old childhood models and painful memories, I love having these beautiful drawings in my room. She did one of the two of us from a selfie we took at the lake and I put that one on my nightstand. It's the first thing I admire each morning when I wake up and the last thing I see before I close my eyes. I can't remember having such a fun summer. I'm not thinking about Dad all the time, just thinking about Natasha.

With it being the last weekend before school starts and me not working, I invite Natasha over to finish her baking practice projects with Mom before the festival next month and suggest she stay for dinner and a Netflix marathon. The alluring scents of sugar and cinnamon mixed with apples fill the air. Buddy's nose is twitching with excitement while we wait to sample their creations.

I taste everything and rank the apple turnovers as my number one choice with the apple crisp a close second. Natasha beams with pride as Mom and I heap our praise on her for the delicious treats.

"I'm off for the evening," Mom says, after we've cleaned the kitchen, along with every crumb of turnover in sight. "If you can't get me on my cell, you can call the café—I'm sure the staff there will know where Molly and Ginny are—those girls are always checking up on the place when they're not there."

We say goodbye, but I am so pleased she's gone—this is my idea of a perfect night, next to the girl I can imagine spending the rest of my life with, along with my best and most loyal friend, who at the moment is relaxing with his head on Natasha's lap. With Mom off for the summer, she's been great about letting us take the van or giving us a little freedom, like tonight, when we can be alone together.

Natasha leaves me to select a movie and pads into the kitchen. As I look for the remote on the coffee table, I notice the message light on my phone blinking. The screen comes to life and shows a voicemail from Dad. "I wonder when he called?" I say to Buddy.

Hey, Toby, it's nice to hear your voice. If you get a minute give me a call back. I'm, uh, not in the field any longer, so anytime works.

That doesn't make any sense. He's always in the field. Dad sounds defeated. I slide the phone into my pocket, knowing something's happened. I'll talk to Mom about it later.

The salty, buttery scent of fresh popcorn wafts through the house. Natasha totes a bowl that holds at least four giant theater buckets of popcorn to the couch and snuggles next to me. Buddy resumes his position next to her, his mouth within easy reach of the snack he loves to share with us.

I push Dad's call to the back of my mind and take up the remote.

"Evan and I started playing cribbage again." The delight in Natasha's voice is unmistakable. "We're planning one more day at the lake. Dad's going to take a day off this week and it'll be just the three of us."

"That's great to hear. Sounds like you guys are making progress." Natasha is a classic film buff, so I cue up an old Alfred Hitchcock flick. The black-and-white film fills the screen and the opening sequence begins. Natasha rewards me with a quick kiss on the cheek.

Normally completely calm, I notice a change in Buddy. Something Natasha doesn't.

His ears turn slightly, and he looks at me.

A car door slams, and Buddy is up. He sits proudly, just in front of us. Waits.

And then there's a loud knock on the front door. I step to the window and a flick of the blinds reveals Evan's car parked at an angle, with one wheel on top of the curb.

I move to the door, hoping naively that he's here for a friendly visit, but the intense look in Buddy's eyes makes me think Evan isn't here for a chat. I open the door, spotting the rage in his eyes.

"Is Natasha here?" His voice is sharp and full of anger. I feel Buddy move next to me.

Natasha comes to the door, standing on the other side of Buddy, as the three of us fill the space. "Evan, what are you doing here?" Her voice, for once, is brimming with annoyance.

"You need to come home," he barks, his face drawn and haggard, his shorts and tank top hanging loose on his thin frame, his usually perfect hair matted and uncombed.

"Dad knows where I am and what time I'm coming home."

A faint growl comes from Buddy, who is leaning closer to Natasha now. I'm sure I'm the only one who hears it, I'm so attuned to Buddy these days.

Evan shakes his head several times, paces, and pounds his fist on the side of the house next to the door as he mumbles to himself.

"How about you come inside?" I suggest and step to the side, making room for him to come through the door. "We're just watching a movie."

"I'm not coming in. She's coming with me."

"What's wrong? Can't we talk about it?" asks Natasha, her voice laced with concern and a slight tremble.

He slams his fist into his hand slowly. "I don't need to talk about anything. I just need you to come home right now."

"We're right in the middle of the movie. My mom could run Natasha home as soon as it's over," I say.

"I'm not leaving without Dad's favorite little girl," he says in a mocking tone. "You're coming home with me now. I'm not sure what you see in Emerald City here." He flicks his eyes in my direction, giving me a sneer full of disdain. "But he's just another loser who's a great fit for this lame town." He turns his attention to his sister. "Get in the car, now." Spittle flies out of his mouth and his face turns bright red. He's in constant motion, his hand movements exaggerated as he shouts. I notice the veins in his neck bulging as he continues his irrational rants and paces the sidewalk.

Apprehension flashes in Natasha's eyes, and I wish Mom was here so we could take Natasha home in the van. She darts to the counter and gets her purse and the platter of treats she's taking to her dad to sample.

She looks at me and, under the shame, I detect a flicker of fear in her eyes. I step onto the sidewalk and take a few steps toward Evan. "She doesn't want to go with you right now. You need to calm down and go home or come inside and talk. Your dad knows where she is and what time she'll be home."

Evan's eyes bore into mine. "Don't. Tell. Me. What. To. Do," he says through clenched teeth, glaring at me.

I take another step toward Evan, but Natasha puts a soft hand against my chest. "It's okay, Toby. I'll just go home. I'll call you tomorrow." Her cheeks are flushed with humiliation.

I turn and whisper to her, "You've got to quit defending him and letting him control you."

She fights back tears and shakes her head. "It's easier if I just go. He'll calm down and I'll come back later." She tries to distract Evan with the pastries. "Want to try one of these? They're really good."

He shakes his head and flicks the platter to knock it out of her hands. I reach for it and catch it.

"Maybe you should be a catcher instead of the big star pitcher, huh?" Evan continues to shout for her to get in the car as he walks toward the street.

I don't feel comfortable letting Natasha go with Evan, but it's clear she doesn't want me to confront him. "Uh, Mom's not far and she can run Natasha home in just a few minutes." I reach in my pocket and pull out my phone, ready to call her. Mom would know what to do and she might be able to defuse the whole situation.

He turns toward us, even more agitated. "You don't need to call your mommy. It's simple. I'm here to pick up *my* sister. Just get in the damned car." He moves towards her arm and she cowers at his touch.

I try to think, but Evan's agitated state makes me uneasy and my mind is racing. I know the route to their house will take them through town. "I need to stop by the store, can I catch a ride with you to town then?" I blurt it out. If I can't stop Evan from leaving, at least I can go with them.

Natasha's eyes signal her thanks.

"I don't care what you do, but we're leaving right now." Evan smacks the top of his sedan and flings open the driver's door.

Natasha reaches for the door handle on the passenger side and I flick my head toward the backseat. "I'll sit next to him," I whisper. Buddy is at my heels, jumping at me and tugging on the end of my shirt. I point to the driveway and tell him to stay and he sits, concern clouding his eyes.

I know he's only trying to protect me and I feel the same way about Natasha. I've never heard him growl like that before and I know he's concerned. He would never jump at me or tear at my clothes. He's a pleaser, by nature, but I know he has a strong desire to protect me and Natasha. I watch as he does what I tell him and sits on the driveway. He whines, something he never does, as the intensity in his eyes deepens. I feel awful but there's nothing I can do. I have to choose her.

Natasha slips into the backseat and I don't even have my door shut before Evan's foot stomps on the gas pedal. The force knocks my head back in the seat and I pull the door closed. With unsteady hands, I grab the seatbelt behind my shoulder and struggle to insert the tongue into the buckle. After several tries, it latches with a satisfying click.

Natasha's concern is evident, her voice strained as she tries to remain calm. "Evan, quit driving like a maniac. You got what you wanted, I'm coming home. Just relax and slow down."

"Don't tell me what to do." He pushes the accelerator. "Somehow all these years, I managed to get along without you. I don't think I need your input." Instead of anger, his voice is full of despair.

"You don't want to scare her, Evan. She was just saying how much she's looking forward to spending the day with you on the lake this week." I turn and use my eyes to encourage Natasha to keep talking.

"Right, that's going to be great and our last chance before school starts. I bought all the stuff to make your favorite chocolate-chip cookies to take with us." Natasha smiles, but the pitch of her voice is higher than normal.

Evan shakes his head. "I'm not going to the lake. It's a waste of time." His voice quivers and breaks at the end.

"How about we go to the Brick House and grab a pizza or something and just talk this through?" I suggest. "My treat."

"I don't need to talk to *you*. We're dropping you off in town and then we're going home." He turns and scowls at me, his eyes dark and callous. He gives the steering wheel a quick yank, as if to prove he's in charge. Natasha mutters as her platter of treats slides across the car and they spill all over the seat and floor.

"If you don't like it here, you can just go back to Mom," says Evan. Natasha unhooks her seatbelt and bends forward to pick up the crushed pastries.

We're out of the residential area and on the road where Buddy and I walk and enjoy the surrounding fruit trees and green fields each morning. This trip is anything but relaxing and serene. Instead of the gentle sounds of buzzing, chirping, and the whisper of wheat swaying in the breeze, Evan is rambling about her never having time for him, while she's trying to make him understand.

"I ordered us a new cribbage set since we started playing again." Her voice is hopeful, but her eyes dart with wariness.

"I like the old set," Evan says, with a hint of nostalgia.

I turn around to make eye contact with her, but when Natasha goes quiet to pay attention to me, Evan glances in the rearview mirror and sees us. "Turn around and quit whispering."

"Evan, please, just slow down and pull over. Let's talk and figure things out. You're scaring me," she says.

I'm thankful there's no traffic on the road tonight but wish there was a policeman or someone around to get his attention. With no stop signs or lights on this road, Evan is gaining speed.

I grip the phone in my pocket and thumb the buttons with the fleeting thought of calling someone.

As we approach the turn with the bigleaf maple, Natasha seems desperate. Evan twists around to look at her, taking his hands from the wheel, tears glinting in his eyes. The car wiggles and drifts to the wrong side of the road and, as he turns back around and yanks the steering wheel in the other direction, the car is headed for the huge trunk of the tree.

There's no time to react, no time to grab the wheel, no time to think. In seconds, the car collides and amid the crunch of metal and shattering of glass, everything turns white and then there is only silence.

CHAPTER 21

Now

I watched, helplessly, that day. I didn't want Toby to go, but there was nothing I could do. I tried tugging on his shirt, but he told me to sit and wait. I whined, sensing danger, but Toby was too focused on protecting Natasha.

As the car sped away, I knew it was going much faster than Toby would ever drive. The car disappeared around the corner and I listened to the engine rev higher. I wish Toby had stayed at home. I can still smell the stench of Evan's sweat—a bitter, sour mixture of anger and utter despair. Something broke in Evan that day and his desperation was palpable, like a fog surrounding him. It was similar to the scent I first detected from Toby, but amplified and more pungent, more hopeless.

Evan reminded me of Toby when I first meet him: he was just a boy. He, like Toby, used anger to show strength, since he believed his other emotions were a sign of weakness.

My heart ached for Natasha as she tried to appease Evan. I heard the longing in her voice when she spoke about him with Toby and knew she hungered for the bond they once shared. She thought things would get better, that they'd go back to playing cribbage. She had a kind heart and wanted to make everyone happy—Evan, Toby, her dad. She was too young to realize and hadn't yet learned that you can't take responsibility for someone else's happiness.

I alternated between pacing and sitting, keeping alert, hoping Toby would return, but the sound of the car faded as it traveled further away from our house. I sat again, in the spot Toby told me to, and the minutes passed by until I heard a horrible sound in the distance. It was so quiet, I could barely register it, but I leapt to my feet. I knew something was wrong; I could feel it deep inside and for the first time since meeting Toby something else overrode Toby's command to stay.

I ran as fast as I could, through the neighborhood, rushing through yards and taking shortcuts, following the echo of the noise. I sprinted by the orchard with no time to savor the sweet aroma of the fruit or nick a fallen apple. I sniffed the air and identified an acrid metallic tang and lots of dust and dirt. I kept moving forward and the odor became stronger. I detected Toby's scent, fused with Natasha's apple pastries, and the caustic odor of metals. My nose twitched as I approached the corner. I gazed at our favorite spot and fear rippled through my entire body. All I could smell was blood.

The beautiful tree where we had enjoyed some of my favorite moments, where I could feel Toby relax as he stroked my head, was now the scene of a horrific crash, littered with pieces of twisted metal and chunks of jagged plastic from the car. All I could think of was my boy and I was frantic to find him.

I reached the corner and through a cloud of dust hanging in the air, saw Evan's car slammed into the trunk of our beautiful tree, the headlights illuminating the wide canopy of leaves. I dashed toward the car and sought out Toby's door—the door I should have never let him close. I stepped on chunks of glass, sharp metal, and bits of bark.

What I saw through the window of Toby's door made my heart sink. The white airbags looked like popped pillows and were limp in front of both front seats. Both boys were slumped over and not moving. Their bodies were covered in fine white dust, their heads slack, and their eyes shut; the coppery taste of blood coated my mouth and nose and the pungent scent in the air grew stronger.

You know how the world stops and things stand still sometimes? That's what I remember from that night. I recall whining and barking as I tried to rouse them. I remember the world standing still. I could only glimpse Natasha's legs and one of her arms, in the back of the car, but she didn't budge either.

I was frantic to get to Toby and I don't know how I did it, and I've thought about this many times. In life-altering moments, everything freezes and when you need to act quickly, your body responds while your mind catches up, remembering for itself the things it must do. That survival instinct. I focused on Toby's face.

I couldn't tell you how long I stood over my boy, willing him to wake up, nudging him with my snout, ignoring the scent of his blood mixed with the dirt and grass I love. My nose twitched at another scent—a sharp odor.

Toby's index finger on his left hand moved and I saw his eyes start to flicker open. Worried he'd close his eyes again, I used my tongue and licked his face, hoping to initiate a response.

Toby's eyes popped open, darting from side to side, searching for understanding. He saw me and the tense muscles in his jaw relaxed and I felt some of his fear ease. He started to move and screamed out in pain when he used his right arm. I followed his eyes to the gaping wound, with jagged bones protruding. He held his arm across his chest with his left hand. His breathing increased and he started to panic.

I wiggled as close as I could to him, intent on keeping him warm and calm. His eyes fluttered and I began licking him and barking, pawing at his pocket where I knew he kept his phone. He had to call for help.

I'm sure, even now, as I wait for my boy, that what I heard him whisper that day, was "Natasha."

CHAPTER 22

Then

You know when you're underwater? Some noises are distinct—the taps are suddenly louder, the dripping from the showerhead, the rushing water around your arms when you submerge yourself in a lake—and some are muffled. I hear people talking above me, but it's like this. My body feels heavy and I sense something tightening on my legs. Sometimes I make out a few words, but mostly it's beeping and soft shuffles. I'm more tired than I've ever felt and while a sliver of light seeps under my eyelids, I can't make myself keep them open.

Minutes or hours later—I have no sense of time—the noises intrude again and seem louder. I crack open one eyelid, just a bit, and the bright light makes me close it again. I must be dreaming. I don't recognize anything. I sense a huge lump in my throat and it's so dry it's killing me. I need a drink of water, but I'm too tired to lift my head and try to find one. The thought evaporates as I sleep again.

A shrill beeping sound infiltrates my dream and upon waking I swallow, delivering a raw and burning pain in my throat and chest. I have to get some water. I strain to open my heavy eyelids and squint at the bright lights and take in the soft colored walls, where still nothing looks familiar. I close my eyes to block out the glare as my head swims with dizziness. Where am I? I can't ignore the pain in my throat, but my head is too fuzzy to get up and find water.

I hear Mom's voice and realize she must be on the phone. A few seconds later, her hand touches mine. I smell the lavender lotion she always wears and open my eyes just a slit to find her standing next to me. She whispers, "Toby, Toby, it's Mom. Are you awake?"

My throat is too dry to speak. I move my head a fraction of an inch and am overcome with nausea. Mom is pale and has dark circles under her eyes, her graying hair flattened on one side. Worry is etched on her face. Mom rubs my hand and says, "You're in the hospital." Her voice is soft and calm, but hesitant.

I try to process what she's saying and take another look around the room. I notice the television mounted on the wall and look down at the blanket covering me and notice the rails along the bed. I frown and give Mom a quizzical look. Her lips begin to curve and the tension in her jaw eases.

A figure stands behind her and I squint to make it out. I blink a few times to focus my eyes. I must be hallucinating. Dad.

She continues to hold my hand and talks slowly. "You were in a car wreck and you had to have surgery on your arm. We're about an hour away from home. You're going to be okay."

She reaches for a glass of water and puts something cold to my lips. "Take a sip. I can get you some ice chips, if that sounds good."

I suck in the cool liquid and let it sit in my mouth. It's soothing and I take several more sips. It hurts to swallow, but the moisture helps. Each time I move my head to drink, a wave of dizziness comes over me. I close my eyes to stop the room from spinning and keep the queasiness at bay. I try to take a deep breath, but don't get far before the pain causes me to moan. I try to speak and only a squeak comes out. I start to use my hand to imitate a spinning motion, so Mom knows I'm dizzy, but can't move my right arm. There's a cast encasing the length of it. I use my other hand and gesture to Mom.

"The doctor said you'll be groggy. It's from the anesthesia and the pain medicine they're giving you." Mom points to the bags of fluid hanging around me. I look and follow the plastic lines that feed into the back of my left hand.

She says she'll be right back with ice chips and I watch her blurred figure disappear out the door. As I close my eyes in an effort to comprehend what she's told me, a firm hand grips my left foot and I smell something familiar—woodsy. It sounds like my Dad's voice, but I can't concentrate and feel myself drifting away. I dream of Buddy barking and pulling me out of a car.

*

Mom is sitting in a chair reading with one of those tiny lights that clip onto her book. The lights are off in the room and my head is less foggy. She glances over to me and smiles. "Feeling any better?"

She moves and brings the water glass with a straw to my mouth and lifts up my left hand to guide me to hold it. I take several long swallows. "Yeah," I say in a croaky voice I don't recognize.

"How's Buddy? Where is he?"

"Buddy is home and missing you. Molly is watching him and has been sneaking him down to the café, so he's not lonely." She pauses and says, "Do you remember what happened?"

I shake my head and say, "Not really. I keep dreaming about Buddy pulling me out of a car. Is that what happened?"

She pulls her chair closer to my bed, puts the water cup on the tray, and holds my hand in a tight grip. "Buddy was there, but I don't know if he pulled you out. It was Evan's car. Apparently, he was driving you and Natasha? That's what the police have said. He was driving too fast and overcorrected. The car crashed into a tree."

An image of giant leaves overhead flashes in my mind. "The bigleaf maple?" The idea of it gone stings me.

She nods and rubs my hand. "Right. His car struck that massive trunk, with the brunt of the impact on the passenger side." She moves her eyes to my right arm, concealed in a green cast.

The shade of green reminds me of our school colors and baseball, and then I gasp and turn to look at my mom. "Natasha?" I watch my Mom's eyes turn watery. "Where's Natasha?"

Fat tears slide down her cheeks and plop onto the white sheets of my bed. She shakes her head and says, "I'm so sorry, Toby. Natasha's injuries were too severe. She didn't survive."

*

I have no sense of time. I wake up and Mom is in the chair, reading again. I've never thought about the sort of radar moms have, but she turns to look at me as soon as my eyes open. I'm relaxed, unable to lift my arms, and I feel heavy and blank—empty, detached. Memories keep poking at me as I watch her come to the side of my bed.

I look into her eyes and I know I wasn't dreaming. The memory of what she told me is haunting me. Natasha is gone. Mom bends closer and touches her forehead to mine, but I don't want to hear. I don't want to know what happened; I don't want it to be true. I hear the words I know she doesn't want to say as I watch tears fall onto her cheeks.

My eyes burn with tears and I'm too weak to fight them. I can't imagine my life without Natasha. It can't be right. She didn't deserve to die and I can't bear to think of her gone. Images flash through my mind as Mom and I cry together, and I close my eyes tight and see Natasha smiling on the boat, kneeling down to cuddle Buddy, and grinning with delight as I tell her how much I loved her drawings. Our first kiss at the marina, the fireworks over the lake where we held hands and watched, the time we rode our bikes to the vineyard and had a picnic under the stars, our last kiss, they all flicker through my mind like frames on a reel of film. The images seem so real, I reach out with my left hand to touch her, but she disappears, like a waft of smoke. Natasha—the person who's made me feel whole.

I can't face this and feel myself succumbing to the overwhelming urge to run away—to escape this horror. I haven't known her long, but it feels like I've known her my whole life. We had plans and now she's gone. She never got to learn to do pottery. She didn't get to enter her apple turnovers in the festival. A flicker of hope flashes in my brain. Maybe Mom got it wrong and she's at a different hospital or Mom misunderstood. Natasha is young and strong and could survive.

"Are you sure?" I whisper. She doesn't say anything, just dips her head and squeezes my hand.

How am I supposed to go on without her? I'll never look into her soft eyes or feel her delicate hand in mine. How can I live without hearing her laugh and seeing her smile? As my mind tries to reconcile the reality, my heart shatters. I can't do this. My tears have turned into sobs and each one delivers a sharp blow to my side.

I take a deep breath and grimace as the pain from my ribs radiates through me. "It's my fault," I whisper.

I shouldn't have gotten mad at Evan and tried to put my foot down, then Natasha wouldn't have felt she had to step in between us and go with him to calm us both down. If I knew my choices that day would bring us here, I would have fought to stay in the house. I never would have let her get in that car.

The painting on the wall is all I can focus on. The soft pastels, the sharp edges, the cheap wooden frame. The image of a lake, like the one in the middle of town, is so blue at the deepest part, it's the same color as Natasha's eyes. The lifelike needles of the pine trees remind me of the drawing she did of Buddy with the wisps of fur on his ears and I remember her hand brushing against mine as she showed me how she blended the colors. I close my eyes and fresh tears leak from them. My mind begs for sleep and despite hoping it's a nightmare, I know when I awaken, she'll still be gone.

CHAPTER 23

Now

It's been another week and Karen begs me to come home each night. I know she's lonely and worried, but I can't leave. My legs are weaker and I'm sleeping more. Each time she comes, she brings different foods to tempt me. I'm not hungry and have no interest in food, not even fresh chicken. I'm only interested in Toby and will wait right here until he comes.

My nose twitches at a familiar scent in the air, one I haven't smelled for a long time. I lift my head and let the air travel through my nostrils. The sweet aroma evokes memories of Natasha and her hair in my face when she bent over to stroke my neck and ears. I know Natasha's gone. I knew it that night in the car, but the emotions the scent carries are strong. I look across the grassy plots and a flash of hope makes my heart flutter.

A few minutes later, soft footfalls in the grass make me raise my head. The familiar smell of Natasha is overwhelming. "Hey, Buddy," he says, stretching out his hand to my nose. "Do you remember me?"

How could I forget him? The boy who made fun of me and Toby the first day we met. The boy behind the wheel of that car. In a split second that terrible accident destroyed so much for so many.

But the person who causes something like that, his life is changed forever.

When I first met Evan, I knew his confidence camouflaged his insecurities, his doubts, and anger. It's difficult for young boys to show their vulnerable side and Toby and Evan suffered greatly because they were too scared to do that.

Watching your family break apart is devastating. Children, like dogs, rely on someone else to care for them. When parents aren't there to provide a safe and stable home it's natural to feel abandoned. There's nothing worse than feeling you don't matter or you don't deserve care and attention.

It's easy to understand how children can think their parents have put their own interests above those of the family, and teenagers, already on the brink of detaching from their parents, would pursue more independence and rely less on their influence. To pull away. But it's too early to do that. It's so important to grow up slowly. I know that better than most.

We all want to feel safe and secure, to have someone to rely on. To have a family who will take care of you and help you when we need it. People who will always be there, in the good times and bad. We all need that sense of belonging, where you can be yourself and not be afraid, where you're surrounded by love and accepted, no matter what you've done. Knowing you'll always have someone to support you, help you, celebrate with you, and cheer you on, gives you the confidence to try new things, secure in the knowledge that you'll always be cherished and welcomed. Having that bond dissolve and being powerless to change it isn't easy.

I haven't seen Evan for a very long time, smelled his scent, or felt his pain and sadness. Sometimes you have to fall down, lose everything, to rise up and turn your life around, and finally find something to live for.

After the accident, my heart broke as I watched my boy become a shadow of himself. He could only focus on what he had lost and his future, which had been so bright, had dissolved into a dark hole. When he lost Natasha, he also lost the strength in his arm, his scholarship, his future, and he felt every new loss deeper than the last.

If humans were dogs, they wouldn't worry about the future. I think that's the main reason we're happier than humans. Living in the moment there's no time for regrets about yesterday or angst about tomorrow. It means you take what you have right now and embrace it. I know it's not easy for humans to focus their attention on today. They have more responsibility and obligations, but I did my best to help Toby experience moments of joy in the midst of his despair.

For dogs, this comes naturally. That's why we gravitate to every bush and tree, we explore and sniff whatever we encounter. We might bury a bone for later, but chances are we'll forget about it until we find it again and it will be a happy surprise. We don't worry about what might happen, who might abandon us. And Natasha's death was just another way Toby learned that people could leave.

When Toby and I would walk together on the way to school or when I'd meet him on the road, he would approach the world more like I did. He admired the blossoms on the fruit trees, the early ripening berries along the fence, and the rich greens as the fields came to life each season. When we played together, his mind emptied and focused on throwing and encouraging me to retrieve.

Coach drilled it into him, to concentrate on one play at a time and not get too far ahead and worry about the next batter. While it's important to learn from the past and not repeat mistakes, one can't dwell there or risk becoming entangled and trapped.

Without baseball, Natasha's loss became paramount for Toby. There were few moments of lightness or happiness in his life, only misery. The times I could guilt Toby into going outside for a walk or to play catch in the backyard, the horrible stench of grief lifted; but without something to force him into the present, he wallowed in the torturous area between memories of the past and hopelessness of the future.

Living like that is not really living. You miss the joy in appreciating a perfect day, a delicious meal, the pleasure of cool water on your dry throat, the beauty of a sunset, or the delight in spending time with your best friend. Toby and I made such progress in the time we had before the accident. He had abandoned much of the anger and resentment he had been holding and begun to flourish at school, on the baseball field, and as a young man discovering love for the first time. After the accident, he reverted to his old habits, made worse by the heart-wrenching loss he felt and his overwhelming anger and hostility toward Evan.

Evan opens his hand to reveal a pumpkin dog cookie I recognize from the bakery. "Karen told me you'd be here. She wanted me to come and see you and try to talk you into going home. She's worried about you, Buddy. You're all she has left."

I flick my eyes toward him and then back at the grave, ignoring the cookie. It smells good, but food isn't important right now. We're all dying, so I don't understand the point in fretting about it. I wish she wouldn't worry herself about it either. Humans worry too much about their deaths.

Evan stretches out on the grass and puts his head next to mine. His eyes are full of love. I no longer smell the anger and sorrow that surrounded him. Instead he smells sweet, like Natasha always did. I push my long tongue out and lick his knuckles.

I move my eyebrows, expressing my interest in him. He reaches for me and pets my ears and I shut my eyes and relish his gentle touch. He places his forehead against mine and memories of that night are flooding through him.

I open my eyes and see tears in his. I sense his concern as he runs his fingers over my paws, massaging me. As he continues to caress my paws, I feel his pain diminish. It's my purpose to ease burdens and I've missed being there for Toby, so I delight in comforting Evan. His soft drops of tears plop on my head and snout and I lick at the salty liquid. Evan's voice thickens as he whispers, "Until my last breath, I'll always wish I had been the one to die in that crash."

It's heartbreaking that it took such a tragedy to motivate Evan to change. I remember how he was, but the young man before me is completely different. He's softened even though that regret will always be there.

Maybe that's why he visits me now.

To make up for his mistakes once again.

To say sorry that someone else is lost.

But he's wrong: Toby is coming home.

CHAPTER 24

Then

The first light of dawn filters through the blinds and Buddy snuggles closer, with his head resting next to mine on my pillow. It's already baseball season. My senior year is almost over and I haven't been to school once. Instead of going to class and practicing with the team, I've spent the better part of five months in bed and these last few months torturing myself in physical therapy, talking about my feelings with Dr. Hawes. It's been just me and Buddy at the house.

Dad stops in and takes care of things around the house for us. I wasn't hallucinating when I saw him in my hospital room. He tells me when I'm ready, he'd like to talk to me.

He made sure the bags of pellets were toted inside for Mom all winter and brought us a fat copper bucket that sits on the hearth, so it makes it easy to scoop out what we need. With the growing season starting, he's been concentrating on the yard.

He doesn't say much when he visits, just sits and reads or watches television, runs errands, and even goes grocery shopping. I keep wondering why he's able to take so much time off, and when I asked him about the message he left me the day of the accident, he just tells me it's a long story and I need to concentrate on healing. He hasn't pressed me.

It's just been the last couple of months that I've begun to believe I might survive all of this. Each morning I wake up and think today might be the day when I feel better. Maybe I won't think of Natasha as many times, maybe I won't focus on the loss of my scholarship, maybe I'll feel less out of control. Maybe one day it won't matter that my arm is too weak to throw. That I might never play baseball again.

Maybe one day I'll be able to listen when Coach tells me I still have something: that I'm still smart, that I still have everything I learned from the game.

Maybe one day I'll listen to what Dr. Hawes says about grief.

The thought of being happy makes me feel guilty, but Dr. Hawes gives me hope when she says eventually the intensity of the loss will subside and while it will never disappear, it won't occupy the entirety of my mind.

I've languished in bed long enough this morning that the bright light of a new day fills my bedroom and reflects off the screen of the television on my wall, a gift from Dad to help me pass the time I spent cocooned in my bed all those months. The television I was so intent on getting that now seems trivial. I shove the covers off and gaze at Natasha's drawing on my bedside table. It's my favorite one of us together, both of us smiling, our arms around each other. It radiates happiness and love—our innocence before it and so much more was lost.

Today's the day I've been dreading. My physical therapist wants me to walk all the way to the bigleaf maple, but I'm not sure I can do it. Physically, I'm strong enough and the pain from the bone bruise on my leg is almost gone, my broken ribs have mended, and my arm is getting stronger. My battle today is a mental one.

Buddy stretches next to me, readying himself for our adventure. He's been a constant comfort, always by my side, steadying me as I walk or licking my tears away when I'm too weary to contain them. I run my fingers over him, as I always do when I need reassurance.

I have a sick feeling in the pit of my stomach and part of me is terrified of revisiting the site where I lost so much that night. After seeing the tree shedding its leaves like used tissues when I came home from the hospital last fall, I've avoided looking when we pass by it. That day, as Mom took the turn, I watched as several leaves fell, like the tree was weeping for me, for Natasha, adding to the blanket of brilliant gold and orange under it.

Despite my angst, we set out after lunch and Buddy's joy is conveyed in the cheerful swish of his tail as he trots down the road next to me. These past months, despite the fact that I can't take walks or play catch with him, Buddy has been my loyal friend. He was always nearby, there to comfort me when I needed him, or lend me his back for support when I struggled to walk. His patience far exceeds my own. Seeing him full of happiness like he is today brings a smile to my face and a sense of peace to my heart. The sun and the sweet smell of the blossoms on the fruit trees takes me back to happier days. I'm still much slower than I was before the accident, but the pain in my hip and leg is manageable now.

I try to trick my mind into thinking it's just another day, like all the days Buddy and I would walk this route. It's peaceful, filled with the quiet noises of nature and the beauty of all the plants and flowers coaxed into new life by the sunshine-filled days. We stop at our favorite pasture and I throw Buddy a few balls to catch, using my good arm. He romps and chases them with such excitement it makes me sorry my despair deprived Buddy of all this. With my right arm, I lob a few gentle tosses and he catches them in the air and rushes back to me, prancing with delight.

After a quick stop at the stream for a bit of water, we continue down the road where we first met. The closer we get to the corner, my pulse throbs in my throat and sweat builds on my forehead. I keep my eyes focused on the road ahead and take deep breaths.

Buddy senses my trepidation and uses his nose to provide a gentle nudge of encouragement as we turn toward the tree. She stands in all her massive glory, her bare winter limbs now heavy with leaves opening to offer their protection to any who seek her shelter. We walk over to the vast trunk and I examine it for signs of impact. I find a ragged-looking area that aligns with the height of a car, with some bark missing. I marvel at the size of her trunk, thankful that she's strong and sturdy and didn't suffer more damage. As I study her girth, I realize crashing into her would be like hitting a granite boulder. How naive I was to think a car would topple her.

I look at the red scar on my arm, which has flattened a bit, and compare it to the wound that incised her bark. The tree's disfigurement is imperceptible in comparison. Buddy sniffs and I examine the ground around the tree. There is no sign of the accident, no hints of the destruction of that summer evening when my whole world changed. I trace the thick mark on my arm, knowing it will always be there, that I'll never forget that night.

Buddy lies down next to the tree, in the spot we always shared. He keeps his head on the ground, but moves his eyes upward, urging me to join him in a break. I ease myself down next to him and let out a long breath. Buddy slides his head across my lap. I close my eyes and stroke his fur, enjoying a quiet moment.

My thoughts, as always, drift to memories of Natasha. Despite only knowing her for a few months, I felt such a powerful bond with her. I imagined us always being together and now she's been gone all these months and it still feels fresh. Thinking of Natasha leads me to thinking of Evan and I pull out the frayed envelope I've been carrying in the pocket of my pants.

When I plucked it from the mailbox last week and saw Evan's return address in Colorado written in perfect lettering, as was my name and address, I dropped it straight away—watched it flutter to the floor, and time stopped in that moment. I had been working hard to come to terms with my anger at Evan, but the sight of it threatened to undo everything.

All the things I've experienced—the angry outbursts, the intense guilt and anxiety, my difficulty focusing, keeping myself isolated, and my feeling helpless are all part of my struggle. Dr. Hawes says it is common in people who lose a loved one suddenly.

When I told her about Evan's letter, she suggested I read it during one of our appointments, rather than on my own. She's also the one who advised me to read it several times. It's been the topic of my sessions for the last week. My initial anger quickly turned to grief as I was forced to relive the days before the accident and the agony of every day since.

I open my eyes and look above to the mighty limbs of the tree, like arms spread over me, offering safety and protection. It gives me the strength to open the envelope. I flatten the pages and read the lines I've all but memorized.

Tears plop onto the paper, smearing some of the ink. Evan's words are sincere and convey his heartbreak, the battle he is waging against his own demons, and the incredible guilt he carries for the accident. He tells me he doesn't deserve my forgiveness, but he would consider it a generous act of compassion.

He explains his own struggle with anger and depression and I relate to all he describes and his feelings of being out of control.

I can't imagine losing a sister.

And to feel it's all your own fault.

Over the last week, Dr. Hawes and I have had many discussions about forgiveness. She told me forgiving Evan didn't mean he wasn't wrong, it only meant I could make a choice to relieve myself of the resentment and negative feelings I harbor for Evan. Instead, I could show empathy and compassion for him and in the process of doing that I may free myself from the heavy burden I've been carrying.

I realize I harbor some of the same guilt Evan describes. I've always thought I could have stopped Natasha from getting in the car or could have done something to change the outcome of that horrible night. It weighs on me, and although I'm having a few more good days now, the idea of being free of all the anger and guilt is scary. It would mean she's truly gone.

I stroke Buddy's soft ears, remembering how much Natasha liked to do the same. Natasha's kindness was one of things I admired most about her. She loved Evan, despite all they had been through. I saw the love she had for him, even that night when he was yelling at her. She wanted to help him, to console him, even to protect him. As I read Evan's words again, I know Natasha would forgive him and, for my own sake, I need to forgive him.

As I get to my feet, Buddy stands on my right side, ready as he's been for all these months, to steady me and support me, letting me rest my weight on his back. We take our time heading back home, stopping to throw a few more balls, soaking in the warmth of the sun, and breathing in the fresh scent of hope. It takes me back to those first days with Buddy and when he crouches and darts by me, teasing me with the ball still in his mouth, I laugh with abandon—something I haven't done since the accident.

We turn onto our street and catch sight of Dad's car in the driveway, and I know it's time we finally talked.

CHAPTER 25

Mom's home and she and Dad are sitting outside on the patio. When Buddy and I come through the door, Dad turns and smiles, standing up to greet me, placing a hand on my shoulder. "Hey, Toby." In the stark sunlight, I take the time to study him. His hair has gotten much grayer and his tone has lost its usual bite. He looks older, the lines on his face deeper and more pronounced. As I stand next to him, it seems like he's shorter and he's definitely thinner. He's always been in great shape, with wide strong shoulders, but today, he doesn't seem as stout. Maybe it's his lack of uniform, pressed and tailored and adorned with medals, but the jeans and polo shirt he's wearing are hanging loose. "You look like you're feeling good today." He releases my shoulder and reaches out to pet Buddy's head.

His gentleness still takes me by surprise. I'm always waiting for the harshness I remember so well to appear. He's been absent for so much of my life, but now I'm ready to understand more.

"Remember you said you wanted to talk when I was feeling up to it?"

He nods and his eyes flit to Mom.

As I move to sit down, he surprises me and wraps his arms around me in a firm hug. "I'm so glad you're okay, Toby. I know I haven't been the greatest dad and I'm sorry for that."

Mom pours me a glass of iced tea and slides the plate of cookies closer to me. "Your dad has some things to tell you." She glances at him and adds, "I've got some work to finish up and will be in my room on my computer. I'll leave you two to talk."

She takes her glass of tea and kisses the top of my head on her way inside. Dread creeps up the back of my neck. I might want to speak to my dad but I wish I didn't have to do it alone.

Dad plucks a cookie from the plate and motions to it. "There's more in the kitchen, have one."

Buddy lies at my side between my chair and Dad's. Dad looks down at him and says, "I was surprised to learn you adopted a dog. He's well-behaved and quite loyal."

I chew and nod my agreement, wary, knowing Dad never approved of animals in the house, but relieved I didn't have to hear his reasons.

Dad clears his throat and takes a sip from his glass. "I probably should have told you this long ago, but your mom and I thought it best to keep it from you, in an effort to shield you." He drums his fingers on the table and his eyes convey anxiety as they dart around the yard, avoiding me.

"In the summer before you moved here, there was an incident during one of my missions. Suffice it to say, everything that could go wrong, did." He takes a breath and puts his hand to his head, wiping his brow. There's a nervousness in him I've never seen before, a softness, a sadness. "Several of us were injured and… I watched one of my men, a man I thought of as my brother, die." Dad clenches his hands into fists and releases them, the thick veins bulging. "We were in a hot extraction situation and Rex went back to help one of the other guys who injured his leg and was having a hard time making it to the chopper."

He takes a deep breath and pours more tea from the pitcher. "I suffered a head injury and although I looked fine on the outside, inside things weren't right." He points to his head. "They call it a traumatic brain injury and it caused some cognitive problems. Along with my own issues, I didn't deal with the loss of Rex, the soldier who lost his life. He had a wife and two kids, both teenagers. I just got angrier and angrier." His voice cracks and he shakes his head.

"Rex and I joined the unit at the same time. Not only was he awesome at his job and I could always count on him or leave the unit in his command without a hesitation, but he was my closest friend. We shared things..." Tears fill his eyes as his words catch in his throat. "We witnessed the worst in humankind and the best. We talked about personal things, things I've never shared with anyone, not even your mom. We were as close as actual brothers, willing to die for each other."

I notice his shoulders are slumped and his voice is softer. I've never seen my dad like this. He seems smaller, humbled, and vulnerable, nothing like the man in my memories.

"I felt responsible for Rex's death. Truth is, there's still a little part of me that thinks I could have changed the outcome. We file after-action reports that go through every aspect of the mission and my superiors assured me there was no wrongdoing on my part or anyone else's, just a casualty in action. Going through the events of the day, the tactical maneuvers, the decisions I made, the steps we took as a team, only served as a reminder of what we could have done to prevent it. I had to relive everything. Every time we had to explain made it harder and harder."

I recognize the pain in Dad's eyes and the sadness in his posture. I have a hard time accepting this is the same man I knew before we moved here. He's emotional and fragile, slouching instead of standing tall. I know the pain of losing someone and my heart aches for Dad. I've never given much thought to what he witnesses in his job or how it impacts him and I'm ashamed of myself. All I've done is push him further away. I've said some horrible things to him. If I had only known, it would have helped me be more patient with him.

"I'm sorry about Rex, Dad." His jaw tightens and a tear rolls down his cheek. Seeing him like this, exposed and insecure, is difficult. I worry about his own injuries and what they mean. "How're you now?" I put my half-eaten cookie aside, no longer hungry. The idea of my dad suffering alone makes me sick with guilt. Regret overwhelms me as I recount the things I've done—the ugly words I've said.

He shrugs and says, "I used to have headaches but they've gone, there was dizziness, but that has subsided, and my mood swings have diminished, but I'm not sure I'll ever be the same." Buddy nudges his nose against Dad's leg and earns a caress of his ear. "I know I was tightly wound before this happened, but after the event, I recognize I was out of control more than I was in control. I was told I couldn't be in the field any longer. I felt like my world was imploding, but I understand it now. Sometimes it just takes a little time."

Dad explains that after several months of sick leave and therapy, he was deemed fit to return to duty, but had to take a training instructor assignment, as he could no longer handle being in the field on missions. I know that was his whole world, what he lived to do. I also know what it feels like to have the rug ripped out from underneath you.

I can't imagine him going to a therapist and opening up about anything. I ponder this as we both stare into the yard. If someone like him, stronger than anyone I've ever met, could be hard hit by the loss of his friend, maybe I'm not as hopeless as I feel. It's clear he isn't over the whole thing and it's been such a long time. I kept slipping back into the dark place and it seems like it's taken so long, I just assumed I was weak.

"I've come to realize that the pain of Rex's death will always be with me. It will fade and become less overwhelming, but I'll never forget it." He hangs his head in sorrow. "I shouldn't forget it."

The afternoon fades as Dad continues to drink glass after glass of tea and tell me more about what he's been through since the divorce. I've never seen my dad cry but he wipes tears from his eyes more than once as he describes the roller coaster of emotions, of which I'm all too familiar. We swap stories and he listens to me. We smile at things, we even laugh. We have more in common than I ever thought. I can't believe all of the things I never knew.

Mom comes to the sliding glass door and gives us a quizzical look. Dad invites her over to the table with a wave of his hand. "It's important that you understand the reason I left you and your mom." He eyes search Mom's and she nods.

"After Rex's death and my head injury, things at home seemed to deteriorate. I know I wasn't ever around much, but following that last mission, I resented not being in the field and took it out on the two of you. I understand it now, but at the time I was beyond reasoning and your mom and I talked and decided me leaving was the best thing for all of us. You were having your own struggles, which I know I discounted, and I agreed with your mom when she pointed out that it was going to be impossible to deal with your behavior and anger while I was struggling with my own issues. I don't think it's a coincidence that when you came here, got away from me, your anger subsided, Toby."

Mom puts her hand over mine. "I honestly felt separating you from your dad was the right thing to do at the time. After watching you suffer with many of the same problems your dad had after his injuries, I realize now it may have robbed you of a chance to have someone in your life to help you deal with your grief. He came right here after your accident and wanted to tell you all of this, but it seemed like you were in such a precarious position, we didn't want to risk upsetting you further." Tears cloud her eyes as she pats my hand.

Dad clears his throat. "We thought we were shielding you from more heartache and worry. We actually planned to tell you long before this and I was going to come and visit last summer, but work got in the way, so I had arranged sometime after Labor Day. Then… well, after the accident, those plans evaporated."

Mom sweeps her finger under her eyes. "I felt like I was walking a tightrope and each time I considered broaching the subject of talking to your dad, I lost my courage and didn't want to jeopardize the progress you had made. You were getting stronger and more independent, and I didn't want to do or say anything that would hinder your improvement. I felt like we were hanging on by a thread." Her voice trembles as she fights to maintain her composure.

A mixture of sadness and annoyance floods through me. I know I caused Mom to worry, but I never understood the panic she felt. Stepping away and looking back, I realize now I was so absorbed in my own grief for those first months I spent at home, I never grasped the depth of Mom's distress. All that time lying in bed, consumed by misery, I rarely thought about the impact on Mom. I didn't consider how worried she was for me. Feelings of guilt mingle with traces of annoyance as I grapple with understanding why Mom and Dad didn't trust me or think I was capable of handling the truth about Dad. I should have mustered the nerve to ask Mom about overhearing her talk to Natasha. Had I known, I'd like to think I would have been more sympathetic and less quick to pass judgment on Dad.

"I'm sorry for what I put you through, Mom." I grip her hand with mine. I turn my eyes to Dad. "I wish I would have known what you were dealing with. I think you probably could have helped me and I'd like to think I never would have punched you had I realized what you were going through." Memories of Dad's red face and wild eyes flood through me. His words enraged me and I acted without even thinking. Never once did it occur to me that Dad could have been dealing with something bigger than I was.

Dad smirks and says, "Truth be told, I deserved it. We were both out of control, saying horrible things, feeding off each other's fury, screaming and yelling, but getting nowhere. I shouldn't have overreacted like I did. I didn't mean what I said and never should have treated you that way. I don't blame you for hitting me. Now I understand I was looking to command something, because I felt so lost without my work. It should have never escalated to that point. I had convinced myself if things had gone perfectly and no mistakes had been made, Rex would still be alive. It was my way of trying to control even that."

Did I just hear my dad say it wasn't all my fault and he was out of control? I'm having a hard time believing this is the same man I remember.

Over an early dinner Mom prepares, Dad reveals more details about his life I never knew. He never talked much about his parents or his experiences growing up with them. I'm shocked to learn he is the youngest of five siblings, none of whom he was close to or I remember meeting. As he says this, I recall the old photo albums Mom has and piles of old family photos from my mom's side of the family, but never any from Dad's. He always said he didn't have any family left.

I discover he never knew his father and suffered through rumors that his birth was the result of an affair his mother had. He grew up poor, not just unable to do things he wanted, but impoverished to the point of going to bed hungry more often than he cared to remember. He describes the squalor they lived in and his attempts to keep his meager area in the tiny house clean and organized amid the chaos, including chickens living in their house. They lived in rural Arkansas, where there was little opportunity to work, but he went to work after school in a local diner doing dishes and cleaning, earning a meager amount of money, but getting a free hot meal on the days he worked.

His mother existed on welfare and did ironing for a few people to make extra money. He was desperate to get out of Pine Ridge and the minute he was of age, enlisted in the U.S. Navy because he'd never seen the ocean. His reasons weren't noble and altruistic, instead he saw it as his only escape. His older brother had joined the Marines years before but, sadly, was killed while they were both serving. It's clear Dad hoped to connect with his brother somehow with them both in the military, but he never did. His sisters followed in his mother's footsteps, still living at home, loafing and freeloading on every available charity and assistance program. After all these years, there's still fresh contempt in his words and his intolerance for laziness or lack of effort makes more sense to me now.

With decades old disgust still thick in his voice he recounts his naivety in sending his pay to his mother. When he was granted leave after his first term of enlistment, he returned home to check on his mother and retrieve his savings only to discover she had spent all but a few hundred dollars. I can only imagine how betrayed he must have felt.

But he found happiness in the military when he made it his career. The security, the sense of family, plus the routine and organization he craved were a perfect fit for him.

Listening to him talk about his life makes my heart heavy. It frames him in a different way and leads me to understand him so much better. I only wish he had told me these stories long ago. Imagine getting excited about having access to laundry facilities, clean sheets, and regular meals. It explains his obsession with order at home and his irritation at the slightest hint of loafing. We laugh about the time Dad was convinced I was playing with the hose outside and not rolling it up when I was done. It took me sleeping outside one weekend with a camera to capture a shot of the neighborhood dogs wreaking havoc through the yard and unfurling the hose.

In addition to the stability the military offered, the sparkle in Dad's eyes and the cheerful tone he uses when he talks about the sense of brotherhood and camaraderie he gained from his time in the military make it clear to me that this aspect is the one he values most.

It reminds me of what I found with Buddy. The dog sitting with me now, lined up beside me, lying with his back leaning against my foot. The wonderful feeling of never being alone, of having someone by your side that you can count on. Someone whose loyalty never fades.

Listening to Dad talk about what being in the military meant to him echoes some of the things Coach Hobson told us. He always stressed the value of the team over the individual and that we would only succeed when we worked together, our efforts focused on the same goal. Everyone had a job to support our objective, or what Dad would call a mission.

I recall all the times Coach stressed the importance of taking things one step at a time. One pitch, one hit, one inning, one game. He told us not to get too far ahead, let the past go, not worry about the next play, but focus on the moment. I glance down at Buddy, his heart always in the present and the perfect example of living in the moment. Coach always reminded us that failure was part of the game and that we had to direct our focus on what we could control, not on things beyond our power. He drilled into us that we could control our efforts and our attitude, but little else.

As I think about the tragedy Dad witnessed and is living with and what has happened to me, I realize how true that is in life, not just baseball. I did not have the power to change how Evan drove that night. I could not save Natasha. All I can do now is manage my own reaction and attitude to the horribleness of it all. Dr. Hawes kept telling me this, but until this moment it never really clicked.

Dad turns his attention back to me and explains how the understanding and support he felt from those who served with him gave him something few understand. He tells me, more than once, that the bond of brotherhood is the most valuable weapon to have in the field. I'm exhausted from the walk today and from the deluge of emotions I've experienced processing all of this. Dad's life has been full of more struggles than I presumed.

I hug him, feeling his warmth against my skin, his tired body relax against me, and I know he's been waiting for this for just as long as I have.

Buddy and I get comfortable on my bed and I flick on the television for a distraction. Dad's words tumble through my mind and it gives me a new appreciation for his success and persever-ance. He didn't let himself become a victim and did what he had to do to change his situation and build a future. If he could overcome all of that, it gives me hope that I can do the same.

I get up to get a glass of water, but slow my steps at the soft murmur of a conversation coming from the living room. As I get to the corner, I catch a glimpse of Mom and Dad sitting next to each other on the couch, leaning into one another, their heads almost touching.

I watch as they embrace and opt to slip back down the hall to my bedroom. The moment is significant and I don't want to intrude. I haven't seen them so close since long before their divorce and after the conversation today, I get a sense that although they are no longer married, their bond is stronger.

CHAPTER 26

Dad's been spending more time at the house since we talked. Some of the warmth is back in his voice, and his mood is lighter than I've seen it in years. He's more talkative and has told me a few more stories of his life in the military, more of the happier ones about pranks he and his teammates played on each other. These memories that sound more like summer camp are in sharp contrast to the horror of the operation that led to Rex's death. It helps me understand the closeness he feels for the guys in his unit.

I've been able to focus on some work: engineering projects the school sent to me, homework on my computer, and my eyes drift to a stack of scholarship applications Mrs. Norman sent to me.

School will be out in another month and I'll graduate despite the time I've taken off. Mom and Coach Hobson want me to attend the ceremony and walk with my class, but I'm nervous about the prospect of seeing everyone and making conversation. I don't want their pity, to see their grief, and I'm not sure I can handle hearing about everyone's plans for college.

I just didn't think I'd ever end up working at one of the fruit farms, in the local shops. Deep down I knew baseball wasn't going to work for me, but I did have my heart set on engineering.

Three raps on the door announce Dad's arrival. He calls out and the rustle of plastic bags and kitchen cupboards opening and closing tell me he's been shopping. A few minutes later he pokes his head into my room.

He moves to the bed, and sits on the edge. "Working on your project?"

I click on the mouse a few times, still slower than I was before the damage to my arm, but getting faster each day. "Yep, we're putting the finishing touches on our design for the competition."

"Your mom said it's in Yakima in a couple of weeks. She wasn't sure if you're going to go." He's quiet as I click a few keys on the keyboard. "I was hoping you'd go. I'd like to come and watch it, especially after you've shown me all your design work."

I close the program and turn to face him. I'm not sure I believe what he's saying and can't remember the last time he expressed an interest in anything I had done. It's what I've wished for, but it takes me by surprise. "I've been worried about going. I haven't gone much of anywhere since the accident. It's hard to describe but I feel like everything in the world continued on, except for me. I can't understand how people can still laugh and be happy, and part of me feels like I'll be abandoning Natasha if I venture out and do things."

I flick my finger across the mousepad. "For the first few months after the accident, I was afraid for Mom to leave, always worrying something would happen to her. Dr. Hawes explained it's a normal feeling and happens often when we lose someone without any warning. Thinking about the worst-case scenarios—because I kept reliving the accident—my brain told me if I could lose Natasha in an instant, the same thing could happen to Mom. I was focused on catastrophic outcomes instead of realistic ones. I feel so much stronger now. Those thoughts are nearly gone."

He bobs his head and says, "Trust me, I know that feeling all too well. That's a major part of the reason I had to give up being in the field. You have to have a certain level of confidence," he grins and adds, "some would say arrogance, to lead a team like mine but, without it, I'd put all of us in jeopardy. It took me a long time before I regained that inner strength to return, even as a trainer. I felt like a fraud."

Such humility in Dad is disconcerting. He's always been larger than life, not afraid of anything, tough and powerful. Grief, it seems, doesn't just prey on the weak.

He sighs and says, "I understand what you mean about being stuck. It seems almost disrespectful to move on, so to speak. All I can tell you is you won't be abandoning Natasha, you'll only relinquish some of the grief you carry." He touches his fist to his chest. "She'll always be here, Toby. All the good memories are yours whenever you need them. Even though I know it feels like it, your duty isn't to mourn her and shut yourself off to the world. From what you've said about her, I can only imagine how much she would want you to seize all the opportunities that come your way and do the things that bring you joy."

I wipe my cheeks with the back of my hand and raise my head to find the sheen of tears in his eyes. I can't summon my voice, but reach forward and wrap my arms around his neck, breathing in the notes of citrus and wood that I remembered as a child. The scent that always made me feel protected. These emotions, this closeness I've longed for that I thought I'd never have again, are so comforting, but I'm not sure I trust them. What if I surrender myself and he lets me down again and disappears?

"I'd like you to come to the competition with me, Dad," I whisper.

Dad drives the van into town to celebrate, with Mom riding shotgun, and Buddy in the back with me, and we spend a couple of hours showing Dad Riverside, taking a drive down to the lake and winding through the hills and vineyards. We show him the high school and Mom's school and end up downtown, where we give him a tour around the town square, and pop in to say hello to Molly and Ginny before Dad treats us to pizza and ice cream.

I haven't been downtown since the accident but having Dad by my side makes me feel stronger. I've been afraid of how I might react to the impact of all the memories of places I'd enjoyed with Natasha. Places that would never feel the same. It's as if I'm seeing it for the first time as I listen to Mom point out landmarks and I take in the charm of our quaint town, the gazebo surrounded by the blooms and greenery of spring, the water trickling in the fountain, people out and about laughing and enjoying the beautiful evening.

The taste of my favorite ice cream, and Buddy's delight when he licks his own cup clean, reminds me of Natasha, but instead of the sadness I feared, it makes me smile thinking of her and how much I cared for her. Like Buddy, being with her made me feel stronger, not alone, like we were partners.

Dad compliments Mom on her choice in Riverside, remarks how welcoming the town is and tells her he likes seeing her happy. I've never heard him talk to her like that, with such admiration. It's wonderful to witness them getting along and enjoying each other's company. Maybe the one good thing to come out of the accident and all this mess is that it helped Dad.

Our family outings the last few years were always so full of angst and stress that we tended to avoid them. It's obvious Dad worked on more than his more recent traumatic events when he went through therapy. Hearing snippets from his life and listening to the raw emotion in his voice, it's apparent that for years he has been holding on to the anger and resentment he developed. It colored his entire life. It makes me realize I don't want that to happen to me.

Molly urges Mom away to the back of the café to look at some new craft idea she has, and Dad and I, along with Buddy, end up down by the marina, staring out at the water. He points at the boats and comments on their equipment and strong points.

It's the first time I remember him relaxed and enjoying himself in a long time.

"You seem so different, Dad. Good different, more at ease."

He turns and nods, putting a hand on my shoulder. "I feel that way, Toby. It was a long road to get here and I'm still working on it, but I'm making progress. I let so much of what happened when I was younger weigh me down throughout my life. I never really let it go. I didn't realize it until I started talking with the doctors after Rex's death. I dealt with it the best I could and thought I'd put it all behind me, but it was still there, poking at me in the recesses of my mind. Dealing with all of it was one of the toughest things I've ever done—harder than what I did most days in a warzone. When I heard what happened to you, Toby—I knew I had to take that final step."

I listen as he describes some of the methods he employed to combat his problems, what was diagnosed as PTSD, many of them the same ones Dr. Hawes prescribed for me. He admits he thought it sounded like a lot of psychobabble when he started and didn't have much faith, but he stuck with it and kept going to his appointments. He talks about the importance of staying in the present instead of slipping into the past and getting stuck there or worrying about the future. "The thing that made the biggest difference for me is finally recognizing that feelings are always temporary."

He rests his hands on the railing and gazes across the water. "Life is always changing and nothing stays the same. The intense sorrow and grief we experience when we lose someone will dissipate, with time. The overwhelming joy and happiness we experience when we win a state championship," he turns and winks at me, "will fade. None of these feelings last forever."

I feel Buddy's nose against my leg and glance down at him. He allows himself to be distracted, always in search of something new, never lingering on any one moment, any loss, for too long.

I let Dad's words sink in as I watch the light from the sun shimmer atop the blue waters. "Feelings are powerful and can become all-consuming. That's why it's essential to remember they are temporary. My therapist told me it's important to keep this in mind, and in happy times, we need to cherish each moment and immerse ourselves in that joy. Those wonderful memories will carry us through during the tough times. When we suffer heartaches and sadness that seem unbearable, we have to remind ourselves that what we're feeling won't last forever. Even though it seems like they will. If we don't focus on the temporary nature, we risk getting stuck there."

Dad's eyes begin to water. "I'm so sorry about Natasha. I know how I felt about Rex and can't imagine your sorrow at losing the girl you loved. It's not easy, but tell yourself what you're feeling isn't permanent, treasure your happy memories with her, and let go of the grief before it eats you from the inside."

The sting of tears burns the back of my throat and I'm not ashamed to let Dad see me cry. We wander down the pathway to the pier over the water and sit on the edge. Both of us tap the wooden deck, swinging our legs slightly in unison. Dad takes a breath. "I learned I can't let my emotions define me. I know they're temporary and I now realize how important it is to let go of the anger, resentment, and fear, or risk having them control me. That's what I did for far too long."

Dad pulls his wallet out of his pocket and plucks a card from one of the slots. The edges of the plain white card are worn and grayed. He shows it to me and says, "My therapist gave me this. It's a good reminder."

I run my eyes over the black text.

Enjoy the good things in life and when things are bad, take comfort in knowing it won't last forever.

Dad raises his brows. "Simple advice, but something I didn't have figured out until recently. He takes another card, a crisp white one, from another slot and hands it to me. "For you," he says, "so you won't forget."

I nod and slip it in my wallet, sensing a closeness to my dad I've never experienced. He grips my shoulder and we watch the sun dip closer to the horizon.

CHAPTER 27

Graduation is a blur of caps and gowns, smiles and happy faces. I would be lying if I said it wasn't hard—if I didn't see Natasha reflected in the faces of my peers, sadness in the things people said to me, as much as I tried to hide it. But I could see how much it meant to Mom for me to walk with my classmates and get my diploma in person. She's worked so hard since we've moved to Riverside, to give us a fresh start, and she's made us a life here.

Somehow, I even get to accept an award for my Martian-based robotic vehicle in the engineering competition.

We invite people over after the ceremony, and they don't stay long, except for Molly and Ginny, who cooked all the food and stay late visiting with Mom outside, gathered around the patio table covered with candles. But something is on my mind all day.

"I've been giving things some thought and talked to the people at the credit union and your mom. I plan to continue working for the next few years and if you can settle for an in-state college, I think I can swing paying for your tuition."

Dad had told me his plans that morning.

I've spent hours making calls, building spreadsheets, narrowing down my options for an engineering degree, tracking costs and requirements. I've thought about our visit to Boise State and realized that it's a team I really crave.

I've read so many pages of information and weighed all the pros and cons of each institution and I know what I want to do. Now, all I have to do is tell Mom and Dad.

*

Saturday morning the aroma of fresh cinnamon rolls and coffee wakes me. When I emerge from the shower, the melody of Mom humming in the kitchen drifts down the hallway. As Buddy and I round the corner, I smile at the familiar sound that has been absent for so long.

"Morning, Toby," she says, giving me a peck on the cheek. She glances at the clock. "Your dad should be here in a few minutes. I thought we'd have breakfast on the patio, it's such a nice morning."

As I help her tote the plates and cutlery outside, Buddy rushes to greet Dad as his telltale boots heavily hit the porch and he knocks on the door. Mom pours two cups of coffee and an orange juice for me as we sit down to the spread.

"Wow, Karen, you've outdone yourself. This all looks terrific," Dad says, spooning fruit next to the warm pastry dripping with cream cheese icing.

After a few bites and small talk about the condition of the lawn and Mom's desire to add some bulbs to the flowerbed, Dad turns to me. "So, what's your news? You said you made a decision about college."

I take a swallow of juice and clear my throat, giving Buddy a gentle rub across the neck.

"First, I have to tell you how much I appreciate you offering to pay for college. It's like a giant weight has been lifted from me. I was worried about what I was going to do and as much as I love Riverside, the employment opportunities are slim. Engineering is what I love and believe is my true calling."

"The suspense is killing me," Mom says, laughing.

I smile back at her and take a breath. "You know I've been researching all my options these last few weeks." The fresh hope in their faces makes me hesitate. I don't want to disappoint them. What I've been contemplating has been weighing on my mind, and if I've learned anything through this ordeal, it's that I have to share my feelings and not keep things locked inside.

"It's no secret I'm devastated at not being able to go to college on a baseball scholarship and pursue my engineering dreams, but I know what I want to do next."

Dad's lips begin to curl into a smile and Mom is almost bouncing on her seat with anticipation.

"I've decided to join the Corps of Engineers." They can't mask their confusion as they both frown at me and then look at each other. "I know it's not something we ever discussed, but I realized, without baseball, what I've been missing is being part of something bigger than me, that sense of team and belonging."

I explain about the research I did and that I could get my degree paid for by serving, plus gain other valuable experience and contacts for a career when I'm finished. I turn to Dad. "Until recently, I've held a negative view of the military. It never crossed my mind to consider serving. I think I've resented your work, blamed the military for you having to be gone so much of the time. I always thought your sternness came from your work."

Sometimes I felt like Dad treated Mom and me like we served under him. I always said he "barked" orders, like we were supposed to jump to attention. Being around him felt stressful, like I was waiting for the next reprimand for not doing something right and I attributed all of that to being in the military.

"After listening to you talk about your youth and what the Navy meant to you, Dad, your affection for it and the soldiers you serve with, I can see I assumed things that weren't true."

Dad nods and his eyes urge me on, while I take another swallow of juice and continue tentatively; I don't want to scare them with this but I know it's the right choice. "I understand that satisfaction you get from being part of a team, something more than you. It's part of what I loved about playing baseball, working together with the other guys. Along with all that's happened, losing Natasha, having my scholarship evaporate, I've been feeling lost, afraid, and alone. I know I need to find a path forward and something positive in my life. The camaraderie and brotherhood Dad talks about hold a strong appeal for me. I need that companionship. I need that purpose, plus it's a way for me to get my degree and build a future that includes engineering. It's the perfect place to get my education and practical experience along with providing that sense of alliance that fulfills me."

I look between them.

Dad squeezes Mom's hand and says, "I can tell you've given this a lot of thought. I think it's a fine idea, Toby, if you're sure. I know you understand the commitment and have no doubt you'll excel at anything you pursue. I could make some calls if you want?" He looks over at Mom for guidance. Pauses. "Find out if we can get you in to see a recruiter so you can ask any questions you have. I could take you myself?"

Mom's reply is a little more hesitant, and it's obvious why. "I understand the desire to be part of something bigger than yourself, Toby. I know baseball was much more than a game to you and it makes me proud to know just how highly you value a college degree. I just want you to be sure and think it through. It's a dangerous time in the world."

"Your mom's right, Toby. Take your time. But we trust you. You're more capable than I ever realized." Dad places his hand over mine. "You've grown into a fine man and I haven't even been here to witness it."

He and Mom look at each other, smiling. It's a beautiful moment, one I've never seen before, them agreeing—for once. She bobs her head several times. "He's strong and smart. He'll get the best training in the world."

I shake my head at Mom. "I'll think about all of this, Mom, but in my heart something just feels right."

Silent tears glide down Mom's face, but she nods her understanding.

Growing up in our house, it's safe to say neither of my parents expected me to choose the military as a career path. My announcement shocked both of them, but they each had a different perspective. For Dad, it was a good kind of surprise and a decision with which he could relate. The pride in his voice and his enthusiastic grip of my shoulder and a hug told me all I needed to know.

Mom's words that sounded like she'd swallowed sand, her rapid blinking, and the way she constantly rubbed her left pinky finger with her right hand, conveyed her apprehension.

Mom has always been a thinker. She doesn't spout off with the first thing on her mind. She's diplomatic and tactful, and likes to study things before judging. After my breakfast announcement yesterday, I left her with a binder full of information about the Corps of Engineers and all that the military offers. Dad has the advantage of having lived it, but I knew Mom would have all sorts of questions and I wanted to give her time to digest the information.

The three of us hung around the house, Dad and I did a few odds and ends, and Mom kept to herself in her bedroom, reading the pages in the binder I had prepared. When it was time for bed, they were still sitting out on the patio, she cradling a glass of wine and Dad sipping his iced tea, their heads close together as they talked. About me? About them?

I've been lying here, thinking about my decision and the impact of it on Mom and Dad since well before dawn. I shift my legs and Buddy stirs from his slumber. We pad down the hallway, amid the soft muffle of snores from beneath the thin door of the extra bedroom next to mine. Dad's car still parked on the street confirms the identity of our overnight guest. Although the kitchen is quiet, the coffee maker is already brewing and the rich aroma drifts through the house. It always makes me think of Natasha and her fondness for it.

Buddy has breakfast while I take care to insert the pages I've written over the last few weeks and slip them into an envelope, writing Evan's address on the front of it. It took me several days to compose a reply and I revised it more times than I can count, but after reading it once more last night, I knew it was ready. It's time. I rummage through the junk drawer and find a stamp and motion to Buddy that we're taking a walk. Always the optimist, he grabs a baseball in his mouth for the journey.

We make the trip to the mailbox near school and when I let go of that ten-ounce envelope, it is like letting go of a bag of bricks around my neck. A weird sensation courses through me, one I can only describe as freedom. My steps lighter, we hightail it back to the road and squeeze through the fence into the pasture, getting in a few games of catch while the grass is still damp with dew. The sun shining in the cloudless sky promises a warm day and by the time we get home, Buddy is panting and I'm in need of a drink of water.

Mom is sitting in the kitchen, drinking coffee, snacking on leftover cinnamon rolls. After guzzling down a tall glass of water, I pop a roll in the microwave and answer Mom's question about where we were. "Just walked down to mail a letter and played a bit of ball."

She raises her brows. "Evan's letter?"

I nod. "I finished it last night."

She moves to hug me. "I'm honored to be your mom. That took such courage."

"It feels good, like I can start fresh." As Dad comes around the corner with the paper, I retrieve my plate and settle in across from his chair.

He looks up above the top of his no-nonsense readers and asks, "What's on the agenda today?"

I shrug and Mom says, "I'm going to spend the day with Molly and Ginny. I need some time to think about things and let all this sink in."

"I'm free until later this afternoon. I'm meeting Lyle and Chet."

A smile brightens Mom's face and softens the worry in her eyes. "You can take the van. The girls are picking me up."

As soon as the sound of Molly's car fades down the street, I turn to Dad. "I know Mom's concerned about my decision. Did she say anything last night?"

He chuckles. "She said plenty." He pours himself another cup of coffee. "She's worried about you, like every mother I've ever met whose son wants to enlist."

"Part of me is nervous, but I'm mostly excited. With the exception of joining the baseball team, it's the first time I've decided something on my own and it just feels like exactly what I'm looking for. I could do something I'm good at and make a difference."

"She'd rather you go to college first and delay your decision to enlist."

"I don't think she understands this is bigger than college, it's more than that," I say, giving Buddy's head a stroke.

"Give her time, it's fresh and you took us by surprise. It's not something that was on her radar. She's thrilled at the progress you've made and was so excited when we talked about a solution for your college tuition. This whole last year since your accident has been tough on her and she's only just begun thinking about you leaving for college. It's hard for her to let you go. You are her whole world."

It's always been Mom and me, but this last year while I've been struggling, she's been the sole person in my life and her life has revolved around me. She'll be on her own when I leave. Even though

Dad's been gone most of their married life, she's always had me. I run my teeth over my bottom lip and nod, not trusting my voice.

Dad grasps my forearm and says, "I know what you're feeling. Although I couldn't wait to leave my childhood home, I wrestled with those same emotions. You've got the courage and strength to do anything you set your mind to. Look what you've accomplished already."

"You're not worried about me, like Mom?"

"I care about you, but I'm not worried about you. If you do go, I know the level of training you'll get and, with your skills, I have no doubt you'll have the ability to conquer whatever they can throw at you. For your mom, it's different. She has no experience outside of mine and it wasn't exactly positive for her. She wants what's best for you, she's just not sure this is it. Deployment sounds frightening to her, not exciting. She's not adventurous, she's more of a planner, so the unknown isn't the least bit exciting for her, it's scary."

I frown and realize there's more to Dad than I ever thought. For the first time, I see them not as my parents. I think about Dad's youth and the courage it took for him to withstand all of it and then enlist with no support whatsoever. He was on his own and made a solid career he loved, albeit one that dominated all our lives. I'm sure Mom didn't set out thinking she'd be on her own most of her life, raising me and taking care of everything. I understand how my choice would be more than a passing worry for her.

"I'm ready for a new beginning and the adventure is part of the draw, but what you said about brotherhood and that idea of having each other's backs, that's what I really want."

There's a faraway look in Dad's eyes. "Outside of family, it's the strongest bond you'll ever share."

CHAPTER 28

I'm surprised at the speed with which the whole process moves. Dad called his connections, and they answered all of our questions, and Mom spent her time in the yard, planting and weeding, baking, and visiting with Molly and Ginny. I gave her space and didn't force her to talk about things. I knew the last thing she needed was pressure but she approached me eventually.

"I've been doing a lot of thinking." She sighed, "I've done little else over the last week." Her eyes moved to Dad beside her, and then locked onto mine. "I can't pretend I'm not worried about you going off to God knows where, but your dad has answered all my questions about what will happen and how things will work when you're in basic training and then move on to the specialized training. I've read all the information you put together, which was well done." She gave me an approving smile, one I've seen so many times when she's praising her students' work. "I respect your decision."

She nodded at me. "I'm thrilled that you're excited about the future and I admire all the effort you went to in making your decision. I'm more than proud of you." She ran a finger under her eye and added, "While I can't promise not to worry about you, I promise I'll always support you, no matter what."

Would I still go if she hadn't approved of my choice? Told me she was glad I had found my path, was excited for my future?

Deep down, all I've ever wanted is her to be proud of me.

I'm nervous, but excited to take the first step toward becoming an engineer. I'll be gone for ten months to receive advanced training in Missouri.

And the hardest thing? The golden retriever sitting by my feet. I can't imagine not seeing Buddy for almost a year and can't even think about leaving him for who knows how long once I finish my training. That is going to be the hardest part of this journey. After talking with the recruiter, I decide to pursue a Special Forces Engineer Sergeant path, where I'll undergo extensive training in demolition, construction, and combat training. I explain the injury to my arm and that I have been released for normal activities with no restrictions. Despite my explanation, the recruiter asks the staff doctor to examine me and to my relief, he deems me fit for the program. This path gives me the most experience across engineering disciplines and provides the greatest opportunities.

After my training, I could be utilized in the United States for projects, but will most likely be deployed for a stint in the Middle East. Dad assures me I'll be able to handle it, especially with all the training I'll get, plus the help of the brothers in my unit, and for the first time in my life, I know I've made my own choice, committed to something, surrendered myself to an experience that will transform my life.

It's my last day with Buddy and we do all the things he loves. After playing catch in the green pasture, we take a long walk to the river and he splashes and swims. On the way home, we treat ourselves to ice cream and stop and rest in the shade of the bigleaf maple. I give him a bath, stroking him as I dry him with towels, teasing him with them and tickling his belly. After he's almost dry, I take great care in brushing him, pouring my love into every stroke as I assure him I'll return.

I tell him how much he's meant to me and that I'll be hard-pressed to find a friend and companion like him, but that I'll think of him while I'm gone and count the days until we're together. He has no idea how much him being by my side has helped me, from the moments when we first met, the walks we took, to the months when I couldn't get out of bed.

I might be anxious about the demands of the training, but after talking to Dad, I know I'll be prepared and able to handle the work I'll be doing. It's unnerving to leave all that's familiar and do something I've never done, but it's also exhilarating.

As I continue to groom Buddy and apply the paw pad cream he likes so much, I remember the fear I experienced moving to Riverside, unsure of what it would bring, and then trying out for baseball, when I'd never even played the game. It turned out to be something wonderful and unexpected and, despite my nervousness, I know in my heart this new adventure is the right one for me.

I try my best to explain to Buddy that I have to go away for a few months and that he'll need to take good care of Mom while I'm gone, and I'll be back to visit when I'm done training, before I get my assignment. When I thought about leaving for college, I didn't account for how much I'd miss Buddy. Mom could have brought him to visit if I was in Boise, but now there won't be opportunities to be with him until I get some leave next year when I'm done.

Buddy has always wanted what's best for me and I know he understands this next step is something I want. Something I need to do. I'm glad he'll be here with Mom while I'm away and can keep her company.

I know how much he'll miss our routines and time together and it breaks my heart to leave him, but I know I have to do this. Here I am, the last night I'll be sleeping in my own bed for a long time, holding Buddy next to me, breathing in his scent, letting his soft fur soak up my tears. If only my recruiter could see me now, he'd probably nullify my application. I put my head next to Buddy's. "I love you and I'm not sure I can do this without you."

Buddy nudges my head with his and licks the fresh tears on my cheeks. The calmness in his eyes tells me he understands I'm not choosing to abandon him. I'll miss Mom and Riverside, but I'll miss Buddy most of all.

I wipe my hand under my eyes and whisper, "I'll be home soon, Buddy."

CHAPTER 29

Now

I feel myself fading and know I won't be able to stay here much longer, but each day I hold on to the flicker of hope that still burns inside me that Toby will return. I resist the urge to close my eyes for the final time because I have to see my boy again. I rest my head on Toby's baseball glove, relishing the scent that carries my cherished memories.

The mornings are getting colder and the harvest is over, meaning winter will be here soon, and it feels just like the first days when Toby left. Karen comes to visit me each morning and afternoon and she is growing weary of my defiance of her desire for me to come home. She knows I'm an independent dog and have gone where I wanted, when I wanted, since the first day she met me.

I've had my share of owners since that first couple who took me home from my littermates. I rode in the back of that truck to Riverside for hours. My owner was here to pick up boxes of fruit to take back home and I wandered away while he was loading. He called for me a few times, but I had never really felt a part of his family and I knew there was somewhere else I needed to be. With Toby.

When I'm not asleep, I imagine myself with my boy. I remember resting on his bed, atop his soft blankets that smell like him, and it gives me comfort. Scents evoke the strongest memories and things that harbor Toby's essence, like his old baseball glove, and his bedding, soothe me. When I get a whiff of Toby or something that awakens a memory of him, like the fruit trees and fresh grass, I think of all the games of catch we played and how I loved watching him play ball.

I spend most of the hours of the day dozing and my favorite dreams are of our time together walking along the road with the freshwater stream and the verdant fields coming to life in the spring. I miss the fun of stealing a few berries from the bushes and the sweet crunch of apples from the orchard.

Sometimes I even dream he's walking toward me where I'm waiting. I revel in the huge smile on his face and run to meet him.

Baseball had a way of teaching Toby the things I longed to vocalize. He learned to fail, without giving up, to concentrate on the present, the moment.

It took all of what he knew to refocus Toby on a path that would fulfill him. And it took finally speaking to his dad.

Dogs don't harbor ill feelings or wait to settle a disagreement. We tend to take immediate action, whether it's the sheer joy of play or the quick bite or nip at an aggressor. We don't leave anything unsaid. It's simpler that way and part of our focus on the present. We live our lives without regrets, because we've poured everything into each moment, each day, each year we're given.

When Toby decided to leave, it broke my heart to watch him, but I understood his desire to be part of something that would give his life meaning. Sitting by the dugout, watching Toby thrive and grow on the baseball field were my happiest moments. I sensed how unsure he was at those first practices, but it didn't take long for him to start believing in himself. With each pitch, his skills improved and his confidence grew. I know what it's like to be lonely and Toby had been feeling that way for longer than even he knew. Having Coach believe in him gave him the courage to take that first step, open himself up, and discover the gratification that comes with being a member of a team.

Not only did he learn the nuances of the game, so graceful it resembles a dance, but the possibility and the hope of being greater than the mere sum of the talents of the players propelled him to achieve more than he thought possible. Toby hadn't been forced to make too many decisions on his own, and the few he did weren't the best. Along with making dozens of decisions during each inning, baseball offered Toby the opportunity to become resilient. He had a tendency to give up: on people, on himself, but with Coach's guidance, he mastered how to recover and learned that failing was just part of the game.

Toby learned he could rely on others, not just his mom, and when he figured out his teammates depended on him, trusted him, cared about him, that's when the magic happened. It opened Toby to value and respect the differences in people and to what I predict are lifelong friendships with young men like Lyle and Chet. He was in the center of the exciting buzz of electricity that existed within the team and it was something he wanted to experience again.

I understood that desire to be part of something, and despite the sadness I felt when he left, I recognized his longing for what he had lost when he had to give up baseball and believed he would find that same sense of belonging in the Corps of Engineers. He didn't just aspire to go to college and study, he thirsted for that closeness that only comes from a shared alliance. Trusting someone else. Feeling worthy.

With such a strong connection to Toby, I'm confident he's still alive. If our bond had been severed, I would know it. I still feel him and have every confidence he'll return to me. That day the men in uniforms came to the house to talk to Karen is burned into my memory. She grasped the couch and collapsed in a torrent of sobs and tears when they explained Toby's unit had been ambushed and that he was missing and presumed dead. That's a weird term that doesn't make much sense. I know it's been months since they delivered their heartbreaking news to Karen, but I'm not willing to give up on my boy. Just because Toby is missing, doesn't mean he's gone.

I'm comforted by some of my favorite images of Toby from my daydreams. My muzzle isn't whitened with age and I leap into the air, just like I used to in the field, and catch every throw, running to him and jumping into his arms. I love those dreams, but when I wake up, I realize I'm still alone, my jumping days long gone.

Toby gave me the best years of my life. I packed in more fun with him in the three short years we had together than the other six before I met him.

After he left, I filled my days walking our same routes. I resumed my old spot in the trees on the edge of the baseball field and watched the new crop of boys practice and play. I loved the deep sound of Coach's voice and the familiar thwack of the ball being hit.

William visited us several times and brought me one of my favorite toys—a bright green frisbee. He took me to the lake during the summer and always took time to play catch with me. It wasn't the same as a baseball, and he's not the same as Toby, but the distraction was welcome.

When William visited, Karen's mood lifted and she acted like she did when Molly and Ginny were around, smiling and laughing more. I think they missed each other and their shared love and concern for Toby provided an excuse for them to spend time together. William had an uncanny way of showing up about the time the lawn needed trimming and would take care of any little household chores Karen needed done while he visited.

Having him around was nice, but the best days were when an email or letter from Toby arrived. Karen used to read out Toby's letters and emails to me. About training, his tired and worn muscles, how he never had time to play catch anymore—even if I was there—and though I couldn't be with him, these moments meant so much to me.

He couldn't say much about where he was, but shared his impressions of the terrain and climate. He always told us how much he loved us and missed us and that he'd be home soon. I looked forward to those communications and could always tell when a new one arrived by the wide smile on Karen's face when she checked her email. But it's been months since Karen has smiled like that.

I know Toby will return from his time in the military, to Karen, to Lyle, to me; he will have gained confidence and he'll be a part of a whole other team. He could fix or build anything, from a simple link in one of Karen's necklaces, to designing machines and vehicles on his computer. He thrived on figuring out how things work and fixing them when they broke. I remember when the sprinklers kept going crazy and I was soaking wet from the hours he spent testing everything and figuring out the problem, having to replace a valve and the controller. His natural ability to tackle a problem and find a solution will serve him well while he's away.

When I allow myself to fantasize about Toby's future, I imagine him meeting a woman who, while she won't be able to replace Natasha, will fill the absence that he thought could never be filled.

I fear I won't be here to arrange a meeting with someone, like I did before.

As I struggle to open my eyes, I notice today is one of the most beautiful days. The sun is shining in the clear November sky, making it seem a bit warmer than usual. It would be a perfect day for walking and enjoying the best of fall, but I can't summon the strength to raise my head, much less walk in the thick grass. The pain in my hip is worse today than it's been and I stretch and bask in the sunlight hoping it will warm my bones and muscles. Just that bit of movement makes me pant.

I shut my eyes to rest and the breeze wafts over me, delivering a familiar scent. I force myself to lift my head and twitch my nose and then wriggle it faster and faster, forcing the scent through my nostrils. I sniff the baseball glove and while I smell Toby, it's not as strong as the scent I detect today. The scent I've been waiting for all these weeks.

I let my nose guide my eyes and gaze across the grassy acreage. I make out a lone figure in the distance and recognize the gait and stance. Am I dreaming again? I blink my eyes several times to assure myself I'm awake. The man begins to run toward me.

I wag my tail as hard as I can.

Tears of relief fill my eyes. I knew my boy would come if I waited for him. He always comes for me.

As his arms wrap around me and he cradles my head in his lap, I relish his soft caress, filled with love. I long to jump onto him and bury my head in his shoulder, but I simply don't have the strength. I knew he hadn't gone.

"Buddy," he says, with all the love and affection we share.

Through watery eyes, I savor the smile of the man my boy has become, listen to his voice, saturated with love, and it fills my heart with joy. I shut my eyes for the last time, content, in the arms of the boy who has been my whole world.

EPILOGUE

Five Years Later

I breathe in the fresh air, carrying the familiar and comforting fragrance of the first blossoms on the fruit trees and the tangy, earthy scent of the new shoots of wheat and alfalfa in the fields. There's a tug on my arm and I grin at the furry wiggling golden puppy at the end of the leash.

"Rookie, no pulling." I gaze at Emily and smile. "Don't worry, he'll be fully trained by the time our son is born, I promise." The ultrasound yesterday revealed we're having a baby boy. My first idea for a name was Buddy, but that garnered a swift veto from Emily. I suggested the name Randy, in deference to one of my baseball heroes, Randy Johnson, who pitched for the Seattle Mariners for many years, and she didn't reject that, but I reckon we're still in negotiations.

She rolls her beautiful brown eyes and grins gently. "I guess I thought you'd be better at training a puppy." She laughs.

"In my defense," I begin, remembering how easy Buddy was, laughing at the idea I had anything to do with it, "Buddy was a grown dog when I met him. I've never trained a puppy before." An image of the one I had been promised when I was just a kid comes to mind. "I did get a puppy to sit for me when I was about ten years old, but it took about two hours of trying." I laugh.

She raises her brows and chuckles. "Really? So you're an experienced dog trainer?"

They say you should never get a puppy when you're expecting, but I love the notion of my child growing up with a dog. Long walks, hazy summer days, cuddles in the grass.

Walking this road, where Buddy and I spent so many happy hours, makes me think of him. I still miss him and a little part of me is hoping Rookie will fill the void in my heart left by Buddy's passing. Until now, my life has been too hectic to introduce a dog into the equation: getting my degree, studying for my teaching credentials.

We're planning our annual fishing trip on the Columbia River this summer. Turns out fishing isn't so much about the fish as it is about companionship and backgammon—or so Dad says. That man has too much time on his hands in retirement. Talking and playing while we wait for the fish to bite, he's obsessed, and over the moon about the idea of the grandson who'll be with us one day soon.

When Dad turned up at the house with this golden puppy, sporting that bright red collar with a shiny silver tag ready for engraving, I was so surprised. When I stroked his soft head and looked into his bright eyes, it felt right, like it felt with Buddy. Dad may not have known Buddy for long but he knows how much he meant to me.

A photo of Buddy, with his friendly face and kind soul, graces my dresser in our bedroom. I've never stopped thinking of him and all that he meant to me.

Those harrowing times I spent in the Middle East, thinking of Buddy and my parents kept me focused on finding a way home. Endless days, alone and scared, gave me lots of time to think and reflect. I thought about the accident and all that I lost. I lived in such a dark place after that and couldn't find a way forward. I remembered that sinking feeling of hopelessness and knew I hadn't survived all of that to give up.

I felt my dad's presence, alone out there in the middle of nowhere, more so than I ever had in all my years with him. The words he said when he took me to the airport that last time echoed in my mind. Through his watery eyes, his strong voice calmed me. "It's a true privilege to be your dad. This adventure you're off to will be full of excitement and thrills, along with hardships and challenges, and you'll persevere. With your talents and training, there is nothing to stop you. Believe in yourself, Toby, believe in your team." His strong arms wrapped around me and held me close. "I'm proud of you, son, but more importantly I love you. Godspeed."

Dad's words, especially in those weeks I spent alone and scared, kept me going. Knowing Dad had confidence in me, like Coach Hobson had believed in me when I'd never pitched before, buoyed my spirits during some of my worst hours.

I thought back to all the times Buddy, in his gentle ways, prodded me to focus on the moment when all I could grasp was what could have been. Buddy was my guide whenever I felt hopeless. I still don't like to talk about my time at war. Some of the horrors I saw are vivid in my mind and it would have been easy to immerse myself in those struggles when I came home, to think about the brothers I'd lost, the choices I'd made, but instead I focused on the fact that I'd survived and made it home. Everyone thought I was dead and sometimes I thought I was lost, too, but I found the strength and concentrated on actions that would propel me toward home. Coach's words reminding us to leave the mistakes of the last inning or the last play and concentrate on the player in the box rang true.

To escape from that situation and get to safety took everything I had—skills, training, physical stamina, and mental determination. Without the lessons I learned from my struggles surrounding the accident and my dad's battle with similar issues, I doubt I would have made it. Sometimes, after a setback, I reminded myself feelings were temporary and I knew I had to be stronger than those emotions and keep focused on my goal.

The relief I felt that night I was rescued was surreal. Since I hadn't expected to reach the camp I was headed to for several more days, I assumed I was delirious. Instead, I had stumbled into an active operation and a group of Navy Seals nabbed me, not knowing who I was, but I had no trouble recognizing their specialized uniform and the trident insignia I had seen so many times. Protected and surrounded by these strong men, some of whom knew my dad, I felt like I was already home. Dad can now joke with me about the fact that an Army guy had to be rescued by the Navy. The legendary rivalry between the two branches lives on in our family.

Once safe, I thought more of my family and what they had endured being told I was missing and likely dead. I couldn't get back home quick enough.

I steal a glimpse of my wife and my heart swells at the sight of her hand resting on the bump of her midsection while she laughs at Rookie. Despite my initial impressions of Riverside when Mom and I moved here, I can't imagine a better place to raise our son. I'm grateful I listened to Mom.

In all the years I was away serving in the military, I missed Buddy most of all and when I returned and saw him sitting at my headstone, I felt a mixture of heartbreak and pride knowing he had been waiting for me. He's the most loyal friend I will ever have. He was my guardian, champion, therapist, mentor, and guide in a world where I found myself in desperate need of such counsel.

I understood why Buddy stayed at the gravesite for me: he knew I would return. The bond we shared was extraordinary. Along with being my companion, Buddy taught me about loyalty. The memory of holding him on my lap as he closed his eyes for the last time, and weeping for the gentle soul of the dog I treasured, is still fresh in my mind. He lasted only into the evening of the day I got home, but that was all we needed.

It ain't over till it's over.

Many of those same lessons I learned playing baseball remind me of what Buddy taught me. He, too, focused only on the present and didn't worry about the past or the future. He enjoyed every single moment, consuming every ounce of happiness that came his way. I now realize I was worthy of Buddy's love and worthy of my dad's.

As we make our way down the road, I take in the beauty of this place, content that I will make Riverside my home, teaching in Mr. Mills's old classroom, and taking over the team for Coach Hobson when he retires next year. Looking back, there were times I didn't think I would survive or ever find true happiness, but when I gaze at Emily and feel Rookie tug on the leash, I realize everything worked together to bring me home.

I'm not sure I would have found my way here without Buddy. He got me through the best of times and the worst of times, always unyielding in his loyalty. Buddy's spirit will be with me until I take my last breath.

I grip Emily's hand tighter as we approach the bigleaf maple, still standing tall with her massive welcoming refuge of shiny new leaves. As we turn toward the tree, a boy of about ten years, holding the leash of a young golden retriever, passes by. The boy's smile radiates and the dog walks in step with him, listening intently as the boy talks. His dog has the same cheerful curve in his jaw and swagger of his tail as Buddy.

I focus on the two of them, transported back to the luckiest day of my life—the day Buddy found me on this same road. As I watch the two of them, boy and dog, absorbed in their friendship, I'm reminded of the reason everyone deserves to experience the unconditional love of a dog. And I think of the hope only dogs can give.

A LETTER FROM CASEY

I want to say a huge thank you for choosing to read *A Dog's Hope*. If you did enjoy it, and want to keep up to date with all my latest releases, just sign up at the following link. Your email address will never be shared and you can unsubscribe at any time.

www.bookouture.com/casey-wilson

My own golden retriever, Zoe, was the inspiration for Buddy. I lost her a couple of years ago, but spent so many years with her by my side and we enjoyed such a special bond, she is what I consider my furry soulmate. I loved writing the parts of this story from Buddy's perspective. Goldens are so loving and expressive, they make it easy to imagine their thoughts and opinions.

There is nothing like the love of a faithful dog. I've come to realize that although we like to think we select our canine companions, that special dog finds us at the time in our lives when we need the love and understanding only our furry friends are able to deliver. A love like no other and a bond that serves to make us better humans for having them in our lives. If only they could stay a bit longer.

I hope you loved *A Dog's Hope* and if you did, I would be very grateful if you could write a review. I'd love to hear what you think, and it makes such a difference helping new readers to discover one of my books for the first time.

I love hearing from my readers – you can get in touch on my Facebook page, through Twitter, Goodreads or my website.

Thanks,
Casey

          CaseyWilsonAuthor

          CaseyWilsonAuth

ACKNOWLEDGMENTS

Writing a book is often a lonely process and is never complete without the involvement of many people. I'm grateful to work with the terrific team at Bookouture, especially my talented editor, Jennifer Hunt, who shared in my belief and excitement for this book from the beginning. Huge thanks to Kim Nash, a marketing and promotion maven, whose effervescent personality is matched by her passion for books. Both of these wonderful champions are fellow dog lovers, who fell in love with Buddy and made working with them a joy.

As always, my family and friends deserve thanks for their continued support and encouragement and for understanding the many hours I spent locked in my office working on *A Dog's Hope*.

Printed in Great Britain
by Amazon